Killing the Dead

By Richard Murray

Copyright 2014 Richard Murray

All Rights Reserved

All Characters are a work of Fiction.

Any resemblance to real persons

living or dead is purely coincidental

Chapter 1

My knife plunged, meeting only minimal resistance as it slid deep into the man's chest and through his heart. A wave of exultation moved through me, a pleasure greater than any intoxicant or any night of joy with a willing woman. For a short time the darkness that wreathed my soul would lift and I would feel wholly alive and real.

As I stood alongside the table firmly grasping the knife, the seconds ticked by. I was determined to hold on to the feeling as long as possible. The pleasure all too soon began to fade and I loosened my grip. My body shook as the adrenaline left my system. It would be a short while now before the urge would come again. A few weeks, a month or more and my mood would darken. The urge would come, the need for violence and pain. That need for death. For the moment though I was sated.

My eyes opened to the dim light of the cluttered cellar concealed beneath my home. It was hardly an ideal place to practice my hobby, but needs must. It would hardly be possible to wander around outside at the moment, not in these unsettled times. Too many people watching out of their windows, too many police patrolling the streets determined to keep order. I reached for the knife and pulled it slowly out of the man's chest. I never had learnt his name.

I stepped over to the workbench that ran along the back of the cellar; it was piled high with odds and ends and covered in dust. Now the bench held the case in which I kept the tools my hobby required. In an untidy heap next to this case were my victim's belongings. I used his shirt to carefully wipe the blood off of my knife. Then I took a moment to go through his pockets looking for a wallet. His lack of name was irksome. We had just shared the most intimate experience and I felt that he deserved to have his name known.

His pockets contained the usual items that people seemed to acquire as they moved through life. Along with a key ring that held half a dozen keys in a variety of shapes and a trim brown wallet. Within this wallet was a small amount of money, a number of credit cards and his driver's licence. I had to move to stand directly beneath the single light bulb hanging from the ceiling just to be able to make out the name. Josh Taylor.

At last I had a name for my deceased companion. I spoke the name aloud as I savoured the taste of it upon my tongue. Josh Taylor, Mr Josh Taylor. I turned to the naked form and gave a small nod, barely a tilt of the head to his slowly cooling form and offered his spirit thanks for the pleasure I had gained from our short time together.

Happy now that I knew his name, I picked up my most wonderfully sharp knife and humming some half remembered pop tune, began to sever the bonds that had held my Mr Josh Taylor to the table. So intent was I on this task that it took a moment to become aware that someone was banging loudly on the front door of my home.

A sudden panic held me frozen as the noise, muffled as it was down in my cellar became more insistent. Was this the police? Had I been found out? My heart raced and I felt a cold sweat begin. I cursed the lack of windows down here. What had seemed like such a good thing when murdering some innocent man was not so good when I needed to see if my lawn was covered with overly excited officers of the law.

The banging continued I needed to do something. If it wasn't the police, then the disturbance could well bring them. If it was the police, well I would rather be upstairs and able to see than stuck down in my cellar with just the one door in or out.

A decision made, I quickly moved around the table upon which Mr Josh Taylor lay, directly in the centre of the cellar and just about ran up the stairs. I burst through the cellar door into the kitchen pausing only long enough to glance through the kitchen window, noting that my small back yard was clear before heading along the hall to the front entrance.

Standing by the front door, the banging was much louder as the door shook from the blows landing upon it. I could faintly hear what could only be described as a hysterical female voice begging for someone to open the door. It was likely not the police then.

As I reached to open the door my gaze fell upon the knife I still held. In my fear of discovery and subsequent rush to the door, I had forgotten that I held it. It was hastily slipped into the back of my jeans, snug against my rear. It would be fine there so long as I didn't sit on it and cut myself open. I turned the key in the lock and pulled open the door, just enough to be able to see out.

The young woman on my doorstep had her fist raised high, ready to hammer once more against my door. Tears were running down her face. She gave a sob as she saw me. "Oh thank god! Please let me in" she sobbed, as a rather large and distracting glob of mucus ran from her nose.

"What?" Admittedly this was not the most articulate response that had ever been given.

"Quick, they are coming! Please, please let me in" she looked back over her shoulder as she said this and started to push forward.

"What..." I will concede that I may not be at my best when confronted with someone displaying a great deal of emotion. I could see a group of people walking along the road, headed towards the front of my house. Something seemed off about them.

"Oh god they are here!" she cried as she pushed past me and into the house. "Close the door. Quick!"

I really didn't know what to make of this. I looked to the people she seemed to be running from as they stepped onto my lawn. As they got closer I realised what it was that had seemed so off about them. They all bore some kind of fresh wound, with blood specked clothing and flesh. The tall fellow who had moved to the lead was covered head to toe in blood, the majority from the gaping hole in his chest.

It took just a moment to realise that I should do as she demanded and I slammed the door closed, turning the key and stepping back. "What the hell are they?" I asked the empty air, as my uninvited guest was nowhere to be seen. In moments the door began to shake once more under the fresh blows as the gruesome looking people attempted to batter their way into my home. The sounds of their banging against the wood soon filled the hallway. The door wasn't designed to hold against this much force. It wouldn't hold them out for long.

"Where's the back door key?" called a voice from my kitchen. I trotted swiftly along the hall my mind trying with difficulty to grasp at some reason behind the madness that I had just seen. Reaching the doorway leading into the kitchen I was met by the young woman who looked at me expectantly.

"Wait. Seriously what the hell is going on?" I asked, my confusion beginning to turn to anger. "Did I really just see someone who should be dead, walking across my lawn?"

"Yes. Dead people are walking around and eating people. Haven't you been watching the news?" she told me, she seemed to be regaining her composure now that she was inside the house, with a seemingly solid barrier between her and those... things. She had even wiped away that hideous snot that had been dripping slowly down her face.

"If I had been, I really wouldn't have any reason to be asking would I?" I said a little defensively.

"Fine. All hell has broken loose, the newly dead are getting up and killing people, who then get right back up and attack others. The police can't seem to stop them and the TV just keeps telling us to stay inside." she said with a rising note of hysteria. She stepped toward me stopping only when her body pressed up against mine, her face twisting into a snarl. "Now you are all caught up, where are the bloody back door keys!" She positively shouted this, flecks of spittle flying out of her mouth and speckling my face.

"Downstairs in my jacket" I said pointing at the cellar door. Without another word she threw open the door and headed straight down. I stood still for a moment, my thoughts racing. The dead were rising and eating people. I was convinced it must be a joke as it wasn't possible for something like that to happen in the real world.

The group of maimed and bleeding people trying their best to enter my home would seem to indicate that she may be telling the truth. If the dead had risen and were in the process of killing people, they would be a competition I did not want. I cursed as some small part of my brain reminded me that I had a reason for having her stay out of the cellar just as she started screaming. I ran down the stairs.

Reaching the bottom it took just a quick glance to see the former Mr Josh Taylor as he stood naked and pale, blood still leaking slowly from the wound I had made. He faced the young lady across the table where I had left him laid in silent repose. The young lady was screaming whilst trying her best to keep out of the grasp of his flailing limbs, as she navigated the boxes and general junk that cluttered the floor.

She seemed to be stuck at the opposite side of the table, unable to step around for fear of the newly risen Mr Josh Taylor grabbing hold of her. I stood at the bottom of the stairs unobserved by either of the guests in my home. I was faced with a simple choice. This world that I knew and felt comfortable in was crumbling, the dead were rising and the rules were changing.

It occurred to me that it was rapidly becoming unsafe in my home; the resounding noise coming from the front door coupled with the naked corpse – possibly soon to be two corpses – in my cellar meant that I would likely be forced to leave.

Whilst it would certainly be simpler to head out on my own, I would encounter times when I needed to sleep, when I would be faced with tasks that I was unable or unsuited to perform. For that reason I should perhaps save the life of this young lady. Though I was unsure how I would explain Mr Josh Taylor it would be useful to have her in my debt, an ally to help me learn the new rules of this changed world. Besides, I wondered, would it feel the same to kill him once more. Reaching behind my back I took a firm hold and pulled my knife from the concealment of my jeans.

Armed and ready, I reasoned that a blade through the heart hadn't stopped him from rising again, so to stop him would take something more than a slitting of the throat or a stab between the ribs. I stepped up behind Mr Josh Taylor and with one quick movement brought up my knife and with all the force I could muster, stabbed it straight into the base of his skull.

I stood still, holding fast to my knife. My heart beat almost painfully in my chest. From the new hole in the back of Mr Josh Taylor's skull, thick dark blood slowly oozed along the knife blade, pooling against my hand. It wasn't the deep pleasure that had filled me earlier but it was something different, a quieter kind of joy.

It was exciting too, being able to kill whilst another watched. I looked across the body devoid of life once more as it slumped forward over the table and met the gaze of my lady guest. She stared back at me her eyes boring deep into mine. I felt perhaps there was a connection there, a meeting of two like-minded souls. Then she screamed once more.

Chapter 2

For a day that had started so well, it appeared to be rapidly worsening as the minutes ticked by. I had just killed Mr Josh Taylor for the second time today and I had done this in front of a pretty young lady no less. A young lady who for reasons I could understand, just happened to be staring right back at me as she screamed with terror. Added to this, the remorseless banging from the group of apparently undead people attempting with all of their might to enter my home, was bringing on something of a vile headache.

"Hey now, enough of that." I said to the young lady in what I hoped was a calming tone. "You have nothing to worry about. Mr Josh Taylor is not going to hurt you." I smiled, as I attempted to put her at ease.

"You think I don't know that!" she shrieked "Why the hell have you got a naked dead guy in your cellar?"

"Oh." I am certain that under different circumstances I would have been able to come up with some wonderfully imaginative explanation. If not I would have just put an end to her and her questions. However, with my rapidly worsening headache and my desire to gain an ally, I felt compelled to use the truth.

"I killed him." I said. She seemed a little overwhelmed by my candour and sat staring at me with her big blue eyes, mouth moving but no sounds coming forth.

"Why?" She asked, as she finally regained her voice.

"Whatever do you mean?"

"Why did you kill him? Why is he naked? And why the hell is he in your cellar!" she yelled, the sound carrying to the undead currently attempting entry above and causing them to redouble their efforts. "What the hell did he ever do to you?" she demanded.

"Nothing at all." I replied.

"Then why?"

This conversation was going nowhere. "I killed him because I wanted to, he was naked because it is easier to strip a live man than a dead one and it was in my cellar because this was the first convenient place." I told her.

"Now if you have perhaps forgotten, you brought some friends with you to my front door, who are at this moment trying to break into my home and I can only assume, kill us. Perhaps we should leave."

"We should leave! Did you really suggest I would go anywhere with you!" she screamed.

"Why not?" I asked, genuinely curious. It seemed perfectly logical that strength lay in numbers.

"Because you have just told me that you murdered a man. I will be safer with those creatures out there" she said, her eyes darting between myself and the staircase. At any moment I was sure she would make a dash for the exit and I would find myself alone. I couldn't shake the feeling that being alone would be a bad thing during a rising of the undead.

"I know it may not mean much to you but I promise I won't hurt you. In fact," I said as inspiration struck, "if you look behind you on the cabinet, you will find my case. In this case are plenty of knives, take one or more. Keep them with you and you can defend yourself." I told her, adding "if the dead are rising surely it would be a good idea to have someone with you who is capable of killing?"

The pretty lady didn't immediately answer. She stood for far too many long seconds as she glared at me, weighing my words. She took a moment to glance behind her at the cabinet, taking stock of the knives it held.

Finally she stepped back and reached into the case, pulling out two knives. The first was a favourite of mine, 115mm slim filleting blade that would fold down into the handle. The second was a more standard combat style knife, 152mm blade, beautiful black oxide coating and a sheath. She certainly chose well.

"Fine, We can stick together for now. You even look at me funny though and I'll gut you" she snarled, brandishing the sheathed combat knife. She looked quite distractingly dangerous and for a moment I considered taking the knives back. I simply smiled though and gave a quick nod of the head to show my acceptance. I then picked up my jacket from the box where I had carelessly laid it earlier, retrieved my knife from the back of Mr Josh Taylor's skull and headed straight up the stairs.

As I stepped out into my kitchen the worst sort of noise came from my front door. A splintering of wood followed by a crash and a deep moaning as the undead managed to force their way in. I pulled shut the kitchen door and pressed my weight against it to prevent access from the hallway. I reached into my jacket pocket, grabbing hold of the back door keys and throwing them to the woman as she came out of the cellar.

"Open the door. Quick!" I yelled.

She swore and ran across the kitchen as she fumbled with the keys to try and unlock the door.

"Hurry" I called across, just as the first body crashed against the door.

I knew that I wouldn't be able to hold on for long, these undead people seemed extremely strong. I looked around my kitchen for something to help block the door. The fridge would work but I doubted that I would have the time to cross the room and manhandle it back to the kitchen door. No. I was left with little choice.

With a deep sigh I bade farewell to my favourite knife before I reached down and thrust the blade beneath the door. A firm kick against the knife handle wedged it firmly in place, making an effective doorstop. It wouldn't last too long, but perhaps long enough for the two of us to escape.

"All clear, let's go." my companion called before she exited my home, and jogged quickly across the back garden towards the high wall that provided a barrier against entry for all but the neighbourhood cats. I said farewell to my home, my sanctuary, the place where I had lived and slept, as I dreamt of all the delightful things I would do to so many people.

It was time to go. I stepped through the door, retrieving the keys before I shut and locked it behind me. It would take the undead some time to break through both doors. We could rest a moment and I would be able to speak to this lady. I had no real idea what was going on or where we would find a safe place.

By the time I joined my somewhat unwilling companion, she had pulled herself to the top of the wall, hanging with just her head peeking over to allow her to see beyond.

"We have a little time" I began, "perhaps we should introduce ourselves and you can tell me what exactly is going on."

She dropped down beside me and paused a moment before nodding. Then she began to speak. "The news has been saying it's happening all over. It began a couple of weeks ago; some super bug was causing people to get sick. After a day or so the people would die. The doctors couldn't figure out why and no drug they tried seemed to work." She turned and looked at me, "How could you not know this?"

"I don't watch much TV and I was busy looking for someone who would be appropriate for my... hobby." I replied, offering a small smile.

"Hobby. Right, that." Her tone gave a firm indication of how she felt about that. "The hospitals got crowded with the sick and then with the morgues all full, the hospitals were running out of space to put the dead." She sighed and leaned back against the wall, closing her eyes.

"My boyfriend worked at the hospital. He called me yesterday. He was scared; he said that something had changed. The people who had died were starting to come back." She started to cry softly, arms wrapped around her body. I wondered if I was supposed to do something to comfort her.

"He was scared. The dead people were attacking everyone. Ripping them apart and the ones they killed would get up and join them. He was stuck on the top floor of the hospital with some of the children." She stopped talking to take the time to – thankfully – pull herself together a little. She brushed her hand across her eyes wiping away the tears before she continued.

"The last thing I heard was someone screaming that they had broken through the doors when the call ended. He didn't pick up the phone again, no matter how many times I called so I jumped in my car and headed straight for the hospital. I needed to know what had happened to him.

When I arrived, it was chaos. Those... things were wandering everywhere. I couldn't even get to the entrance. The police were there with guns and shooting at them. It didn't seem to stop them. I saw some of the policemen die, dragged under a crowd of those monsters and ripped apart. It was awful. I panicked and drove away." She sighed once more. "I was listening to the radio in the car; it said this was happening everywhere and that people should stay indoors. I was heading home when one of those things stepped out in front of me. I swerved without even thinking and drove straight into a parked car. I had to get out and run, then some of those things started chasing me. I arrived here looking for somewhere safe from them." She laughed a little bitterly at that. "Ironic huh? Running for my life from the undead and I end up in the cellar of a murderer." I had to agree that it was somewhat ironic. I started to laugh at that and after a moment she joined in.

"Well this place certainly isn't safe anymore." I said after the laughter subsided, "and by the sounds of it, we will find more of these creatures all over the place. I think the first thing we need to do is get some transport. Before we go though, you still haven't given me your name."

"Lily. My name is Lily." She said.

"Hello Lily, my name is Ryan." I smiled, happier now. I don't know why but I have always hated not knowing a name, whether that is the name of an object or a person, without the name I can find no way for this thing to fit into place in my world. It is more than a little irksome.

"Ok then, beyond this wall is an alleyway that runs between the rows of houses. At the far end - unfortunately the end furthest from us - are the garages for these houses. We may find at least one car there, though it won't be much use without a key" I said.

"Don't worry too much about that." Lilly said with a smile that transformed her face from pretty to truly beautiful. "I had a bit of a reckless youth. I can possibly hotwire a car if we need to."

This was the first good news I had received since she had arrived at my door. While I could drive a car, the mechanics of them were a complete mystery. I had always preferred the inner workings of the human body over those of the machine.

With a firm plan in mind, we climbed to the top of the wall, Lily with a great deal more grace than I managed. From the top, as we sat on the cold stone we could see towards either end of the alleyway. All was clear along its length. The long stretch of cracked pavement had weeds growing through the gaps. It was filled with broken bottles, food wrappings and the general detritus that people felt the need to dump over the walls. Along each side of the pavement were the garden walls much like my own, occasionally broken with the shadowed recess that indicated a gate set into the wall. With a final look back at my house, we dropped down into the alley.

By unspoken agreement we stayed close to the wall. It seemed imprudent to walk out in the open. I let Lily lead the way as she was the only one with anything resembling a weapon.

As we cautiously made our way along the alley stepping through the puddles of what I could only hope was remnants of the last nights rainfall, I couldn't help but look behind us. The hairs were rising on my neck and I couldn't shake the feeling that we were being watched. I would look up at the houses around us but could see nothing to indicate anything was different today. It was an unpleasant feeling that I wasn't at all familiar with.

We paused as we reached the end of the alleyway. A cautious look showed a row of garages in an overgrown area of dirt. The simple structures were just boxes made of concrete with a metal door that opened outwards, though all were closed. Aside from the alley entrance you could only leave by the single wide ramp down onto the main road. Two cars sat silent and ready to be stolen by Lily and myself.

We cautiously moved along the front of the garages towards the closest car. This was a grime encrusted black rectangle on wheels. Perhaps some alpha male type would have been able to give you the car's make, model and engine specifications. I could simply tell you that it had four wheels, four doors and was fairly small.

Lily gestured for me to step closer as we reached the car. The stress of remaining undetected must have been getting to her as when she spoke it was in a whisper. "Keep a watch for any undead whilst I try and get this car started."

"Happy to do so, however I seem to be without any sort of weapon." I pointed out.

"Ok, take this then." said Lily as she reached into her pocket and pulled out the fold out filleting knife. I wasn't sure what good it would do against the undead but it was better than nothing. I stood with my back against the garage door, allowing me to see both the alleyway and the road entrance just by constantly turning my head from left to right.

Lily, happy that she could work undisturbed pulled off her jacket and bunching it up. She held it firmly against the car window before striking the glass hard with the butt of the combat knife. The sound of the window shattering was muffled and we were extremely fortunate no alarm went off.

As Lily pulled open the door and climbed into the car to fiddle with whatever it was that she needed to fiddle with. I tried to keep an attentive watch though my headache was still with me and I was considering our options.

I was forced to work on the assumption that Lily was correct about what she had told me earlier. The dead were rising everywhere and not just here. This meant we were going to have a great many problems. We had left my house with only the clothes on our backs and a couple of knives. Finding some sort of shelter from these creatures would be important, but getting hold of some supplies was equally so.

Getting hold of the supplies would be the problem. If these undead were killing and multiplying then the emergency services would not be able to cope. The police would be forced to rapidly fall back. This wasn't America. Aside from special tactical units, the majority of the police were unarmed. I highly doubted the undead would be concerned with pepper spray or Tasers.

No. The government would be forced to deploy the military, which would not be easy as a great many of them were overseas fighting on foreign soil. So, with an almost free reign the dead would soon be overwhelming in number. This in turn would mean no food deliveries to the supermarkets, no happy industrious workers turning up at the power or water treatment plants. No one in fact would be keeping the basic infrastructure intact. This presented a rather bleak future for us.

The sound of the car as it burst to life awoke me from my reverie. Lily looked up triumphant, "Told you I could do it." she said with one of those seemingly rare but breathtaking smiles. Her smile turned to a frown as she looked over at the alleyway. "Who is this?" she asked.

I followed her gaze to see a rotund man running up towards us. He didn't seem to be undead and it didn't look as though he were being chased. He did however seem red faced though that could just be from the exertion of running.

"Shit. I think this might be his car." Lily said. "He is going to be pissed at us." I would consider that a problem easily solved. I pulled open the knife.

"What are you doing?" Lily yelled as she noticed what I was preparing to do.

"We need this car; I won't allow him to stop us."

"No. You can't kill him. Rule number one if you are sticking with me. No killing live people." Lily's frown was directed full force at me. I wilted slightly. The rules of this new world hadn't seemed to have changed that much after all. If I wanted to group with others for protection it seemed like I would have to play nice.

"Fine, no killing." I agreed, somewhat sulkily closing up the knife and slipping it back into my pocket. I silently added 'for the moment.'

"What the hell are you doing with my car?" demanded the angry fat man as he finally waddled up wheezing and flapping his arms in an indignant rage.

"We need to get out of here, you do too. Haven't you seen what's happening?" Lily said her tone firm and brooking no nonsense.

"Bah, I don't care what's going on. That's my car and you can't bloody take it," Angry man shouted at Lily. I was becoming annoyed; the shouting was making my headache worse and would no doubt attract unwanted attention.

"Please. It's not safe here and we really need to get away." Lily pleaded.

"I really don't care. Get the hell out of my car." said the angry man as he reached across and grabbed Lily by the arm, hand grasping tight and causing her to yelp in pain.

My knife was out and unfolded in an instant; I stepped up against the angry fat man and stabbed the blade into the side of his leg. He screamed and fell over releasing his hold on Lily.

"What did you do?" Lily shouted.

"I didn't kill him" I said, surprised at how defensive I sounded and how much I wanted to not upset Lily. "We really need to go and his shouting will attract them."

Lily looked at me for several seconds, I couldn't tell exactly what she was thinking but she looked annoyed. I hoped she wasn't going to set off without me.

"Pick him up and put him in the back." Lily said finally.

"Why?"

"Because we can't just leave him lying here, he needs some medical attention." she said looking down at the angry man who lay on his side, hands pressed against the bleeding wound in his leg.

"You stabbed him. You get to look after him" said Lily. "Don't you dare even think of arguing, if you say one word I will leave without you." She punctuated this last word by slamming the door shut and grabbing hold of the wheel.

I resisted the urge to sigh and put away my knife. I grabbed the wounded man under the arms and I was able to lift him, straining slightly under the weight, before I pushed him awkwardly into the back seat of the car. I told the man quietly to keep hold of his leg to staunch the bleeding before I closed the door and trotted around the car.

"So where to?" Lily asked, as I climbed into the passenger seat beside her.

"I have an idea." I said. "First though, we need a library."

Lily spared a moment to glance my way, one eyebrow raised in silent query. I gave her my widest grin. I had a plan. Seeing that she would receive nothing further from me and with no place of her own in mind, she nodded once and we set off.

Chapter 3

The journey to the library in the town centre took twenty long minutes. The streets we passed were deserted by the living. The few undead we saw seemingly excited by our presence as we passed through their midst set up a gurgling sort of wail which, coupled with the moaning coming from our passenger in the back seat was extremely unpleasant.

The undead themselves were fascinating to watch. I could recall movies I saw as a child about the undead coming back to life and shuffling around eating brains and such like. These creatures seemed to have no special interest in the brains of their prey, any flesh would do.

As we passed one intersection I chanced to see two of the undead fall upon a young woman. In the all too brief moment before we passed beyond view, I had the chance to see them as they used their teeth to devastating effect. They ripped into her flesh, blood and pieces of meat spattering the ground around them. I was unsure whether or not they would be able to actually digest anything, but they were certainly trying.

Another group of the undead we passed were a mixed lot. The leading fellow in a suit and tie had no wound apparent at all, as far as I could tell. The old man directly behind him was missing a hand and had a large hole where his throat should have been. These wounds didn't seem to inconvenience him in the least. Yet another of the group had such a large hole in her neck that she was unable to raise her head.

It occurred to me that these creatures were truly undead. They didn't seem to feel pain and whilst they did bleed, as proven when I stuck my knife into Mr Josh Taylor for the second time, it was thick and dark and almost congealed. Rigor mortis was likely setting in, which would indicate that the older these undead became, the slower they would be.

I recalled Lily's words from earlier that this seemed to have started with a superbug of some kind. It was entirely likely that the bug was transferred through contact with bodily fluids. My gaze travelled down to my hand, still bearing some of the blood of Mr Josh Taylor. It apparently didn't matter too much if you got their fluid on your skin, but I doubted how safe it would be to get their fluids in the mouth, eyes or an open wound. It would be a good idea to wash my hands as soon as possible.

"We will be at the library in a few minutes. You want to tell me why we are going there?" said Lily breaking into my quiet contemplation.

"The world is going to hell, perhaps literally." I said, nodding towards another group of the undead wandering out of a side street as we passed. "Food will become an issue and clean safe to drink water will definitely become a problem. I personally have no idea how to purify water, how to grow vegetables or what medicinal benefits can be found in the plants that grow all around us. I think this may be knowledge that we will need though and the best place to get that is at the local library." I said, adding as an afterthought "it will also likely have all kinds of maps of the surrounding area."

Lily seemed to consider what I had said, swerving around a gruesome looking corpse standing in the road. I wondered idly if it had any thoughts swirling around in its rotting brain.

"Ok. I see what you mean. It's as good an idea as any I suppose. Perhaps it will have a phone that works inside." Lily said.

I was pleased that she had agreed with me. I had spent so much of my life alone it was an interesting feeling to have someone listen and act on my words. I was so pleased that I didn't bother to complain as she pulled up outside the library and instructed me to bring the angry little man who was now whimpering and bleeding all over the back seat.

The town centre was as deserted as the streets we had driven through. I imagined that if we went by the hospital we would find it a great deal more crowded, but for now I was happy not to have to deal with too many walking corpses.

Lily jogged across to the library entrance as I lifted the angry man out of the car, throwing one arm around him to help keep him upright as I ignored his curses. Fortunately the library was a new building. Two stories high and built on level ground to ensure the elderly and disabled didn't have too many stairs to climb. I was happy for that considering how heavy the angry man was.

Lily pulled the doors open and stepped inside. She stuck her head back out a moment later and motioned for us to join her. Angry man gave a whimper and a new curse word every time he put any weight on his wounded leg. A little more blood dribbled out with every step, which would have amused me more if it wasn't being brushed onto my own leg as I helped him along.

I stepped into the library and heaved a sigh of relief as I dropped angry man on the floor. He swore at me and moaned.

Lily looked less than amused. I felt it prudent to find some way to secure the door and have a look around.

The doors each had a small bolt at the top and bottom which allowed them to be locked tight without the aid of a key. I reasoned that as long as we stayed out of the line of sight of anyone outside then we should be ok.

Lily was busy helping angry man to a chair behind the librarians counter so I decided to wander about. The library was two stories high, the ground floor being almost exclusively books with a few computers for people to use. The second floor could be reached from a set of stairs by the entrance that led up to door for an art gallery of some sort. I can honestly say that I had never felt the need to go up there so perhaps that would be something worth doing.

Lining the sides of the building for its full length were shelves full of books. Through the centre of the room were rows of standalone bookshelves rising almost to the roof, whilst in the centre were the desks and chairs, where the casual reader could look through their books in comfort.

To the right of the doors were the librarians counter and a square office, the plain wooden door was closed. Lily was rooting around under the counter.

"What are you doing?" I asked her.

"Looking for a first aid box, they must have one, it's the law or something, I'm sure." Lily glanced at me, showing her most fearsome frown so far. "We need a first aid kit because someone stabbed Brian."

The formerly angry man who I now knew as Brian was also flaring at me. I felt that perhaps we may have gotten off to the wrong start. "Hello Brian, glad you could join us." I said offering him my most sincere smile.

"It's Mr Johnson to you." Brian said, as my smile faded under his withering glare. I shrugged and walked away, leaving them to it. I made a mental note to look for something I could use as a weapon as I headed for the computers.

The first terminal wasn't in working order; the second though had an internet connection. I sat and spent the next thirty minutes browsing any of the news sites that I could actually access. A great many of them were either running extremely slowly or simple showed an 'error, unable to connect' message. It looked like I was not the only one trying to find some news.

Eventually though I had a working picture of what was happening. The world had indeed gone to hell. In an incredibly short space of time the governments across the globe were calling on people to get off the streets. Not so much to maintain order but to try and stop the undead killing people and adding to their ranks.

The name I had seen bandied about by several news services was Zombie. It made sense I supposed. Undead and walking around eating people would kind of fit most people's definitions of zombie. I wondered why I had been shying away from calling them that. In the end I figured it didn't matter. Zombies were rising and taking over this dreary little world of ours.

According to the news, the militaries of the many nations of the world were having problems. Simply shooting the zombies wouldn't work. The movies had been right about that at least, destroying the brain was the easiest way to kill them. That alone made much of the modern militaries weaponry pretty pointless. Grenades designed to incapacitate or fling shrapnel around would be no use. Blow up a zombie and all you had for your trouble was lots of pieces of zombie lying around and any parts still connected to a head trying to bite your ankles as you walked past.

The BBC at least was working and listed some advice. If you knew someone had been infected in any way – usually by a bite or initial sickness– then you needed to quarantine them. There was no cure. If you could stay in your home or place of business you were advised to do so and the rescue services would get to you as soon as they could. I kind of doubted that one.

If you had nowhere that was safe to go, the military and police were setting up refugee centres in most towns that they could reach with the limited personnel. Generally these would be in schools or sports stadiums as they could hold plenty of people and be secured. The final piece of advice was to avoid hospitals. The majority of these would by now be swarming with zombies.

I leaned back in the chair and digested this. It certainly wasn't looking good. I looked over to see Lily and Brian chatting. It seemed she had found some bandages and managed to get Brian to calm down a bit. It was annoying how easily he could talk to her. Small talk was a skill that I had never really acquired.

Through years of practice I had become used to assessing people as threats or potential victims and Brian was neither. Middle aged and overweight, a handle bar moustache and glasses. He sat there in his beige khakis and flannel shirt. I would have no trouble killing him if required. Though at the same time he was too loud, too likely to be missed if taken as a participant in my hobby. All told he would be someone on the street that I would have no cause to look at twice. He annoyed the hell out of me though and that bothered me.

Lily on the other hand would certainly never have been a victim of mine. She too would be the sort of person who would be missed. Her shoulder length dark hair, beautiful blue eyes like windows into her soul – a cliché but no less true for that - and a smile that could light a room, though I had seen little of that; no, even sitting there talking in jeans and a t-shirt she stood out. She would be missed by far too many people.

At the same time I couldn't see her as a threat, but something about her made me wary. I couldn't help but think that getting too close to her would be a really bad thing for me, though I didn't know why. It was an instinctive feeling though and over the years I had learnt to trust those when I got them.

Shaking off my thoughts of my current companions, I stood and started to walk around the shelves of books. The ones I wanted would be in the reference section which would make the area to search manageable.

I was stood between two of the large shelves searching amongst the books when the smell hit me. It was revolting, something along of the lines of rotting meat mixed with raw sewage. I wondered briefly if the drains were blocked when a rather unpleasant realisation hit me.

The library doors had been unlocked yet we had seen no sign of any of the members of staff who may have opened then. I still had the knife I had used to stab Brian and I took a moment to take it from my pocket and open it up. I could hear Lily laugh at something Brian said back by the entrance and, wary of calling out and alerting any potential zombie, I slowly started to walk back the way I had come.

I was having another 'eerie' feeling, as though someone or something was watching me. I really don't like that sort of feeling at all. The hairs were standing up on the back of my neck again. I swivelled on my heel quickly to look behind me, nothing there. I breathed a sigh of relief and turned back.

Oh shit! The zombie had come around the corner of the bookshelf. A dark trail of blood led from her mouth and down the front of her dress. Her silence disturbed me as I couldn't tell if that was due to some predatory instinct or damage to her vocal cords. However this woman died, the number of wounds she bore told me that she must have been attacked by several other undead.

My blade was raised before me. I intended to wait until she came close enough that I could swiftly drive my small blade up beneath her chin and end her miserable existence. At least that was the plan. As she came around the corner and realised I was there, a ready meal just waiting to be eaten she picked up speed. Unfortunately she had been dead long enough that her limbs had stiffened and one of the wounds on her ankle was too deep. The ankle gave way and the zombie stumbled, her claw like hands taking a vicelike grip on my jacket as she pulled me down with her.

Caught by surprise I landed on top of the zombie, and the putrid smell filled my nostrils. As she writhed beneath me her teeth clacked together as she tried to bite me. I panicked. Knife carelessly dropped as I frantically attempted to push myself away from her bite and get back onto my feet.

A desperate grab for a shelf gave me the leverage I needed and I managed to pull myself back to my feet, as I scrambled to put some space between myself and the zombie as she thrashed about on the floor. Her bloody and broken fingers were scratching against the worn carpet as she tried to take hold of me. Foul creature! I kicked her as hard as I could, catching her cheek. Greying skin split and a dark sticky substance splattered my shoe.

My panic was leaving quickly replaced by anger. This zombie, this pathetic shell of a human being who would have been nothing more than a victim to me just days ago had scared me. Me! I was the one who scared others. I was the one who brought fear and death. I kicked repeatedly at her rotting form as I released all of my rage.

Just a few frantic moments had passed since the zombie had first appeared around the bookshelf. It lay unmoving on the floor, its skull a bloody ruin. I stared down at it and all I could think was how my shoes, covered in bits of brain and gore were ruined. I had no sense of joy, no satisfaction at the taking of a life. I was left with emptiness. Where the rage had been was now nothing, I had become drained of all feeling. I had never taken a life in such anger. It had always been coldly calculated. I hoped that the lack of joy was a reaction to the panic. I could not fathom a world where the taking of even the false life of the undead did not bring me some measure of pleasure.

A low moan rose from the shelves around me. My struggle with the zombie had not gone unnoticed. It would seem she had some friends. I ran out from between the shelves calling out to Lily.

As I sprinted down the length of the library I saw Lily and Brian look towards me, puzzlement rapidly turned to alarm as they caught a glimpse of the zombies pursuing me. Lily vaulted the counter in a display of agility I was sure that I could never match. She ran to the entrance doors reaching to unlock them before she paused, staring out through the glass.

My laboured breathing from just a short run would have been embarrassing any other day. I reached Lily and took a moment to glance back at my pursuers. A dozen zombies were slowly shambling towards us. They were a curious mix of the most gruesomely wounded, with body parts and chunks of flesh missing from their mutilated bodies, which accounted for their lack of speed.

"Open the door Lily we need to go" I said.

"No point." Lily said, her tone one of defeat.

"Why?" I asked as I looked back at her. She was still staring through the glass. Brian had by now joined us and was swearing quietly as he leaned against the counter for support.

More than a little exasperated I reached for the locks myself and recoiled as I finally realised what they had been looking at. Zombies, far too many zombies were walking around just outside our library.

"Well!" I said.

Chapter 4

My - thankfully slow - pursuers had reached the centre of the library. The zombies outside had not noticed us yet, though our car was pretty much surrounded. Lily had perhaps reached the end of her tether. The stresses of the day had taken their toll on her. Brian was just as useless now as he had been when we first met him. It seemed that if we wished to survive for much longer, it would be up to me.

So be it. We had two options. We could duck into the office and see if we could bar the door or we could head up to the art gallery above us. We did I supposed have a third option, but since that would be to be devoured by the slowest zombies in the history of the world. I decided that wasn't really an option.

I took Lily by the arm and gently pushed her towards the stairs. "Come on. Upstairs, we can block the door." She seemed to perk up a little and moved up the stairs ahead of me. Brian hobbled along behind us, sweating and cursing at the exertion.

Happy that Lily was moving up the stairs, I dashed ahead to the door to the gallery. Puffing and panting I decided that if I survived then I would do more cardio. The door was fortunately unlocked. It was also, somewhat more unfortunately just plain glass. We would definitely need to find some way to block it off.

"Ryan." Lily called. "Brian needs help. He can't get up the stairs."

Brian was indeed struggling to climb the stairs. His injured leg couldn't fully support his weight and he had nothing to grab hold of to support himself in the bare staircase. I resisted the urge to roll my eyes and sigh. I consoled myself that if he were having problems, then the wounded zombies may struggle just as badly.

"Fine, I'll help him. You need to find something to block the door up there and check for any zombies first." I instructed Lily as I trotted back down the stairs. Lily just nodded and headed up.

As I reached Brian I risked a look at the Zombies. The smell alone indicated they were getting closer, the moans were getting louder and I had a moment's concern that the zombies outside would hear and come and investigate. The zombies were almost upon us staggering en masse towards the only meal available, the three of us. I heaved Brian up the stairs as fast as I could. I was doing my best to ignore his swearing and glares.

"Curse all you want, if those things reach us I will happily leave you to them. So you better move" I snarled.

Terror gave Brian the adrenaline surge he needed to make it all the way to the top of the stairs, where he promptly fell through the door gasping. His bandage had reddened, fresh blood leaking through. I slammed the door shut.

"Help me with this" Lily called from across the room. She stood beside a large blue couch. It was one of the fashionable seats that made up a small rest area before the entrance to the art gallery proper.

With a grunt I grabbed one end of the couch and with Lily's help managed to get it set before the door. I looked around the room, seeing the reception desk beside the gallery entrance. The rest of the room contained a table and two sturdy looking blue armchairs set beside the space where the couch had stood, a water cooler and a door labelled bathroom that faced the main entrance.

It wasn't much but it was all we had. In just a few minutes Lily and I had piled the table and chairs against the door. It wasn't great but the width of the staircase wouldn't allow more than a couple of zombies to stand at the top at one time. I hoped it would be enough to stop them forcing their way in, at least for a little while.

After a final check of our barricade, I instructed Lily and the ever more useless Brian to stay and watch the door whilst I investigated the gallery. I was determined to ensure that we wouldn't have another surprise. They agreed and I left them as Lily crouched beside Brian and attempted to staunch his bleeding.

I opened the door onto the gallery. It was a large and open space with skylights in the ceiling to let in plenty of light for the art aficionados to properly view the works on display. Hard wooden floors had been polished until they gleamed. The centre of the room was filled with cases that contained sculpted works of art and at the far end of the room were doors leading to a back room. The sign above the doors instructed they were for staff only.

The walls of the gallery were lined with paintings from local artists. Landscapes, seascapes and portraits of a ridiculous number of animals made up the collections that hung on the wall to the left of the entrance. The opposite side contained more surreal works. Splashes of colour covered the canvases. Swirls and shapes that were supposed to have some meaning. It looked like something a child could do. I wondered briefly if more normal people would see something in these pictures. If it was perhaps some flaw within myself that meant the supposed beauty of these works was lost on me.

Dotted around the room were some heavy looking benches where guests of the gallery could rest when overcome by the dazzling beauty and talent of the works that filled the walls. I made a mental note to drag them through to the reception area to help barricade the entrance, after I had broken the rules of the gallery by entering the back room.

The off limits room was a disappointment merely being a store room filled with boxes of odds and ends of art, nothing of use in the event of a zombie apocalypse. It did have an emergency exit which I made a mental note of. I headed back to the reception area, stopping to grab a bench and drag it through with me. The benches were heavy and I was amused to see the great gouges made in the floorboards as I dragged the bench along.

As I walked through the door I gave the all clear to Lily and she helped with the rest of the benches. Before long our barricade was much more secure, the large couch weighed down by six benches, two chairs and a small table. I sat beside the cooler and took a much needed drink of water. With all the heavy lifting, running for my life and zombie splatter, I stank.

I figured that now was as good a time as any to check out the bathrooms and hopefully get a good wash. I heaved myself up wincing a little at the aches and pains that even a small rest had created. I entered the bathroom.

It took only a few moments to see that the bathroom was just a single stall, a wash basin with a mirror and a small window set high into the wall. After checking the stall was clear, I ran some water and washed my hands and face. An attempt at using some damp paper towels to brush off the worst of the mess on my clothes was quickly abandoned. Too much gore, the clothes wouldn't be clean any time soon.

The window was locked so I went back out to my companions and once more gave the all clear. Lily gratefully went to use the facilities whilst I had another drink of water. When she re-joined us we sat in silence for a little while listening to the moaning from the zombies as they tried to climb the stairs.

"So where do you think all those zombies outside came from?" asked Lily.

I had been considering this and thought I may have an answer. "They followed us I would imagine."

"Really, what makes you say that?"

"Well, those zombies downstairs. They were quiet at the back of the library until they realised we were there. Once they knew we were there they came after us." I said.

"Yes but they were so slow" said Lily

"That's not actually that big a disadvantage. They may be slow but I don't think they need to rest, to sleep. I imagine that unless they see something else to distract them they will just keep on going in whatever direction they are travelling, until they can no longer move forward. Then they will wait patiently until they find something else to chase." I said, thinking back to the scene I had glimpsed through the door earlier. "I think that some of those outside were ones that we had passed in the car. We came in a fairly straight line so it's likely they followed along and others with nothing better to do followed them."

"So what do we do now?" asked Lily. She sounded tired.

"It is getting late" I said glancing at my watch. "It will be dark in a few hours. It may be best to try and rest here before moving on tomorrow."

"You can't be bloody serious." Brian spoke finally, "we can't stay here with them out there. We need to get help. I need a hospital too if you hadn't forgotten." The last was said with a glare directed at me full force. I resisted the urge to grin at him.

"He's right though" said Lily indicating me. "We don't want to be out there when it gets dark and we can't go to a hospital anyway. They were worst hit by this." Her eyes filled with tears as she remembered her boyfriend no doubt. Brian was solicitous and hastily agreed to stay when he saw she was upset. It seemed he was as uncomfortable as I with over abundant emotion which was one point in his favour at least.

"It's agreed then. I suggest we all try and get some rest whilst we can." I said, taking off my jacket and folding it so that I could rest my head on the clean inner lining as I used it as a pillow. The others followed suit and we lay for a while, each lost in our own thoughts.

My watch told me that it was after midnight when I awoke. The building lights were still on and the moans from outside hadn't grown any fainter. They were masked slightly by Brian's snores. Lily was gone. I stood and went into the bathroom, knocking gently first. I was loath to disturb Lily if she was within. When no one answered I went in and used the facilities myself.

When I had finished my business and dutifully washed my hands I went looking for Lily. I found her in the main gallery standing lost in thought as she gazed at a painting of a seascape. I quietly walked across the room to join her, careful not to startle her.

"It's beautiful isn't it" said Lily with a gesture to the painting, as I stopped beside her. I gave a noncommittal grunt and we stood in silence once more.

"How many people have you killed?" she asked suddenly, taking me by surprise.

"This morning was my sixth. Seventh if you want to count the second time I killed him." I said, raising a small smile from Lily.

"Why do you do it?"

I thought about how to answer this for a little while. Lily was apparently willing to wait patiently. "I do it because I enjoy it." I said finally. "No other reason."

Lily turned her gaze from the painting and gazed intently at me. "How did you know you would enjoy it? What made you kill your first person?"

"He annoyed me." I chuckled as I thought back to that day two years ago when I had made my first kill. "That is why I chose him. He annoyed me with some small matter of no importance now".

"That's all?"

"Yes. I had been thinking of doing it for a while. I had decided I wanted to do it. Killing someone I mean. I had planned how I was going to do it and where. The only remaining question was who." My memories were surfacing of that day, bright with remembered joy.

"That seems a terrible reason to kill someone" said Lily, frowning.

I needed to choose my words carefully now. I realised that what I said next could scare her away and in just one short afternoon I had demonstrated a remarkable lack of skills for dealing with a zombie apocalypse alone.

"You have to understand. The people I chose to kill were not people anyone would miss. I ensured they were people without close ties, people with no children or relationships. The first man was a drug addict. I had seen him rob some old lady. He just snatched her handbag right there in the street. I was doing the world a favour removing him from it."

"So you only kill bad people, like that guy from the TV show" said Lily brow furrowed in thought.

"Something like that" I said. My thoughts went back to the drug addict. He had knocked the old lady over as he stole her bag. She had the misfortune to fall into me, knocking my cup of tea from out of my hand. It irked me, so I had given chase and eventually cornered him. He had died not for stealing from the old lady but for annoying me. If it helped Lily though, I wouldn't complain.

"I won't tell anyone" Lily told me finally. "Hell I don't even think it matters anymore. For what it's worth though, I won't tell anyone. When we get somewhere safe though, we split up."

"Sure. Whatever you think is best. Provided we can find somewhere safe. I was serious though, earlier today. I won't hurt you."

Lily nodded and moved to the next painting on the wall. "Where think we should go next?" she asked.

"Well my idea was a bit of a disaster but the reasoning is sound. Before anything else we need some food and supplies I think."

"Can we even leave here with those things outside?"

"Sure we can. This place has an emergency exit which should take us out onto a fire escape. Not sure how Brian will do though we should be fine." I said.

"He comes with us. It's your fault he will struggle, so you owe it to him to help." She said sternly.

I just nodded. Brian was going to be a dead weight. The time was coming when I would have to get rid of him. I said goodnight to Lily and went back to try and get some more sleep, confident that in the morning I would think of a way to solve the problem of Brian.

The sound of a radio woke me. I sat up and stretched in an attempt to relieve the fresh aches I had gained from sleeping on the floor. Lily was still asleep, curled up in the foetal position in the corner of the room. Brian was sat behind the reception desk, hands busy as he fiddled with a small radio. A thump from beyond our barricade indicated that at least one of the zombies had managed to climb the stairs.

A trip to the bathroom took care of my first concern. The second would be harder. I was hungry. I hadn't eaten since yesterday morning.

"You find anything to eat in that desk?" I asked Brian.

"No." He replied curtly. He said this with a sneer, lips pursed. I had little interest in conversing with Brian but in an attempt to distract my thoughts from my grumbling belly, I tried to ask a few questions. Brian's responses were single worded and full of distaste. I gave up.

I filled one of the dwindling stock of cups that were stacked neatly on top of the cooler with water and drank. I had read somewhere that if you are hungry and drink water it could fool your stomach into thinking it was full. Three cups of water and fifteen minutes later I just needed to use the bathroom again and was still yearning for something to eat.

Brian had finally settled on a radio station. The sound went in and out on the crappy little radio but we got the gist. The world as we knew it was definitely over. Zombies had been reported in nearly every nation. A few of the islands considered themselves to be clear and had closed their borders.

Our own beloved government had decided that it was time to vacate London for a safer location. The largest cities in England were now considered lost. There were far too many people, too many zombies and nowhere near enough troops to contain the problem. The military in its wisdom had decided to consolidate the smaller towns and cities where it could. People were being advised that help was unlikely to reach them. If you wanted safety, food or medical treatment you would have to risk the journey to your nearest relief centre.

The news started to repeat and Brian started playing with the dial again. "So that's it then." Lily said as she sat up rubbing eyes that had dark rings under them. I wondered how much sleep she had managed. "See if you can find a local station, it may list local relief centres." She instructed Brian who nodded and bent to the task.

With Brian busy on the radio Lily headed to the bathroom. I decided that I had better check the emergency exit. The art gallery was the same, early morning light shining through the skylights. The store room door opened to reveal the dark interior to be quiet and still, dust floated lazily in the light that spilled through the open door.

The emergency exit was the same as any other I had seen. A metallic gray door with a push bar handle. Wary of an alarm sounding when the door opened I checked for any wires connected and found none. The gallery must have been depending on the door itself being proof enough. Minimal security equals minimal cost to the local council no doubt. I cautiously pushed down on the handle and the door swung open.

Beyond the open door was a black steel fire escape. The grime encrusted steps covered in pigeon droppings, led down to a parking lot behind the library building. A few cars that likely belonged to the library and gallery staff were parked in the lot. A large wire mesh on a metal frame formed the gate that presently stood open.

From my vantage point I couldn't see any zombies but a large part of the car park was hidden from view. We would have to be cautious. The exit door definitely opened only from the inside. I stepped back within and grabbed one of the heavier looking boxes and opened the door once more. I placed the box on the fire escape to prevent the door closing. If things went badly, we could at least get back inside.

Exit secure I headed back inside the building to find Lily striding through the gallery purposefully towards me, radio in one hand and Brian hobbling along beside her.

"I know where our closest relief centre is." She said as she waved the radio towards me. "It's the football stadium, other side of town."

"Makes sense I suppose, can fit plenty of people in there."

"So we go there, get some food and some medical attention for Brian." Lily said as she ran her hand through her tangled mess of hair. Brian pressed his lips together, eyes narrowed but thankfully refrained from commenting. "God I wish I had a hair brush." She muttered.

"Okay, well we have a few cars outside. Not sure what else is out there though." I said.

"It will be fine. Here you better take this, I will help Brian." Lily said handing me the combat knife. I immediately smiled. I felt naked without a weapon and the memory of my reaction in the library was not something I wanted to repeat. A weapon no matter how unsuited would give me a great deal more of a chance to defend myself.

"It will be up to you to protect us both." Lily stressed.

"Of course I will be your most valiant protector, have no fear." I announced. Lily rolled her eyes and a small smile tugged at the corners of her mouth. We headed for the exit and down the stairs.

Brian made it down the stairs without incident though he had to lean on the railing for support. Lily was by his side to help him. I stood at the corner of the building looking out over the car park as I waited.

Four cars sat quietly awaiting the return of their owners and two zombies had wandered through the open gate. There was enough distance between the two that if I were careful I could perhaps kill them one at a time. As Lily and Brian arrived I whispered my intentions and instructed them to consider which car they would steal.

The knife I held helped to keep the panic I had felt earlier at bay. I was confident with a knife. It was my weapon of choice and with blade in hand I felt I would be able to defeat any number of these monsters. I crouched down as low as I could and crept to the nearest car.

Zombies were dead, that was one thing I was sure of. That would limit their sense of smell, hearing and eyesight surely. Individually these creatures were slow, their wounds and the likely onset of rigor mortis limited their movements. Speed would work well for me. A group of these things would be a nightmare and with their numbers growing with their every kill that could soon be a problem in a smallish country with other sixty million people.

A glance over the top of the car bonnet showed that I had not been noticed. My chosen target was standing still, unmoving and unfortunately looking in my general direction. My heart started to beat faster as I absently wiped the sweat off of my palms against my jeans. I readied my blade, held so the tip was facing forward with the extremely sharp edge towards the ground, then stood.

The zombie let out a moan that sounded entirely too loud and then he started running towards me, arms reached out as if I were already close enough to crush within its embrace. The fact that they could run was an unpleasant revelation.

I stepped around the front of the car, my timing would need to be right or my time on this earth may well be done. The smell hit first, rancid meat and human waste. The zombie was fifteen paces away, ten paces, five. Its mouth opened revealing broken teeth stained black with the congealed blood of its last meal. Three paces and I stepped forward and to the side ducking beneath the outstretched arms. My blade slashed once quick and sure across the back of its right leg, cutting easily through the material of his pants and deep into the flesh.

No scream of pain or anger. No collapse to the ground. Just a stumble and the zombie turned back to me. I was still crouched and as the zombie lurched back towards me I stood between the arms and thrust my blade up beneath the zombies chin and into the brain.

My heart hammered, blood leaked from the wounds I had made. The once again dead man fell against me. I pushed it away to land unceremoniously on the ground, my knife sliding free of its flesh. I cast my gaze for my next target.

Just a few seconds had passed since the first zombie had seen me. The second, a frumpy middle aged woman in life was alerted by the moans of the first and headed my way. Thankfully a great deal slower than the one I had just despatched.

I stalked forward to meet it head on. No attempt to wound or incapacitate this time. Well rehearsed tactics for killing the living would need to be adjusted. This zombie though was slow and stupid. It stumbled and lurched towards me, arms flailing as if it didn't have total control. It was easy to avoid as I kicked out hard against the side of the creature's leg and heard a crack as the leg buckled beneath it.

The zombie fell, face first to the tarmac of the car park. I watched a moment as it struggled to stand before I kneeled down, one knee pressed firmly against its back. I pushed its head down with my free hand exposing the point where its spine joined with its skull, before striking.

My heart was hammering, adrenaline surged through my veins and I could feel it. The pleasure was there, small compared to how it felt when I made my usual kills but it was there. Lily and Brian arrived breaking my reverie. I would need to be careful. Getting lost within myself after a kill was dangerous out here.

Lily's queries were waved off as I busied myself with cleaning the knife. It was too soon for mindless chatter, too soon for questions. I needed a moment for my body to calm, my mind to quit its racing. So I quietly cleaned the knife as best I could against the clothes of the zombie, taking deep breaths hard as that was to do with the stench that surrounded us.

The faster of the two zombies concerned me. I had no way to tell how long ago it had died but the wound certainly didn't look fresh. If some of these creatures were managing to retain some of the speed and range of movement they held in life, it could be a problem.

An inspection of the corpse revealed their flesh to be cool, much as any corpse would be. The congealed blood that oozed from the wounds I had made was dark crimson with black lumps. The skin itself whilst pale retained much of its colour. This was puzzling.

I thought back to the third person I had murdered. I had been pressed for time and after the kill I had been forced to leave the body for a while rather than immediately disposing of the remains. By the time I was free to return, the body was well on its way to decomposition.

The body had become discoloured, the blood without circulation had pooled and settled. The limbs were stiff from rigor mortis and the body was bloated slightly from the gas created as the body's own bacteria devoured their host. The stench was unbearable.

These zombies stank. At the same time, they were not bloated. Whilst the blood did seem to be congealing it appeared to be circulating around the body. Though, looking at the two corpses before me, it would seem that this worked better in some than others.

Whatever it was that had animated these corpses looked to be keeping the decomposition at bay. If this was the same for all of the zombies then the problem was worse than I had initially imagined. If the zombies decomposed like regular corpses then a year, perhaps two would have seen them pretty much done for.

A decomposing corpse would not bear up well in a warm summer. The insects, scavengers and bacteria would eat them alive or perhaps in this case, undead. The process of decomposition itself would damage the bodies enough that the skin would fall off. The internal organs and tissues would liquefy leaving bare skeletons. We would survive just by outliving the bloody things.

Without the normal decomposition these creatures could be around for a long time. With the rate their numbers were seemingly growing this world could rapidly become populated with nothing but the dead. This was not a pleasing thought.

"We can't use these cars" Lily said breaking though my thoughts.

"Why not?"

"Too new. They have alarms. I don't know enough to stop the alarms going off and that will bring them all running." Lily said, her arms crossed across her body as she hugged herself. Even I could see she was frustrated.

"Well then looks like we are walking." I said, as I stood and tried to brush the worst of the grime from my hands against my already filthy jeans.

"What about Brian?" Lily said looking back to where Brian leaned against the car. He was clutching his leg, pain evident on his face.

"I doubt you are willing to leave him, so we will just have to do the best we can." I sighed. "Let's go."

I set off walking towards the gate. Lily followed behind moments later helping Brian slowly limp across the car park. This was not going to be pleasant.

Chapter 5

Beyond the library car park was chaos. The streets where once the people of the town would walk as they browsed the local shops and sipped expensive coffee concoctions from any of the homogenous corporate stores that could be found in any town, were now almost empty. The shops stood closed and dark waiting for life to return.

Fresh splashes of blood covered the pavements. Broken glass and abandoned cars strewn across the streets. Zombies wandered around, sometimes alone and more often in groups as they hunted for their next meal. In the distance thick black smoke rose high into the early morning sky.

We moved slowly, keeping low and hiding behind abandoned vehicles. Lily would try the door handles as we passed hoping to find one unlocked. She stopped trying them after one opened to reveal a zombie strapped firmly into the front seat. No evidence of what had killed him but he appeared unable to release himself. Lily quickly closed the door lest his moans drew the attention of the others.

As we made our way along the almost empty streets I wondered where everyone was. This was not a small town and whilst the majority of people lived beyond the centre, I was at a loss as to why so few zombies wandered around. An answer came a short while later as a car sped past. The occupants white faced with fear, the car loaded with all they held dear. As the car passed the nearby zombies all turned to follow, seeming not to care that they could not catch it.

The zombies then were moving ever outwards as they followed their prey. The centre of our town would remain almost deserted in parts, whilst the outskirts would be filling with a rising number hungry to feast on the people trapped in the houses there.

Lily caught hold of my arm and pointed down a side street to our left. I saw immediately what had caught her attention. A large silver people carrier was surrounded by zombies, all clawing at the windows as they pushed against one another to get within. I could think of only one reason why they wanted in.

I shook my head at Lily, "we can't help them. That's far too many zombies for us to deal with." I told her in a firm whisper.

"He's right. Nothing we can do lass." Brian agreed, for once being useful though a glance at his pale face told me that it was most likely due to fear.

Lily frowned shaking her head. She seemed to genuinely want to help the unknown people despite the obvious disadvantage we would face.

"Lily listen. We cannot do anything without risking ourselves. There's just too many of them." I said.

She put her hands to her face, shoulders slumped. Defeated. That was the moment we heard the high pitched cry of a small child, muffled from within the car. Lily's head snapped up, gaze locked to mine. Determination filled her eyes. "We have to help them," She said, tone firm and brooking no argument.

My hands moved slowly as they massaged my temples to fend off the headache that was definitely on its way. Refusal would be the simplest and safest option. I could say no and walk away. The alternative would be to risk my life to rescue some people which would be something I definitely did not do without good reason.

Another cry came from the car causing a new surge of activity from the zombies trying to claw their way in. Any minute now one of them would figure out how to smash the glass and the people inside would be dead. My problem would be solved. Lily continued to stare.

"There's a child in there Ryan" she hissed, her arms crossed before her. She wouldn't back down. Truth be told I liked children and whilst I couldn't grasp why the opinion of this woman meant something to me, it did. So I guessed I was about to do something stupid.

"Fine!" I snapped back as I took stock of our situation. Brian would be useless so I discounted him. I had a knife, Lily and after a quick count; eight zombies surrounding a car. The street was empty and lined at either side by various shops. Raised brick planters stood at intervals filled with dirt and a variety of flowers. No weapons and no place to hide. Just wonderful.

Lily looked at me expectantly. I outlined a rough plan then stood and drew my knife. I took a deep breath then moved forward blade held ready in a reverse grip, tip pointed downward and sharp edge forward. I was as ready as I ever would be.

Slowly I crept towards the zombies, body kept as low as possible to avoid notice from the undead. The smell once more assaulted my senses. If I tried to breathe through my nose I wanted to gag. If I tried to breathe through my mouth I could taste the foulness on the air. I settled for taking shallow breaths and resolved to get a cloth to wrap around my face.

When I reached three paces of the car I was still unnoticed. I risked a glance back to see Lily and Brian getting into position. My intention was to strike quickly to kill a couple before leading the rest away. Another deep breath then I stood and moved one step forward as I swung my blade, aimed directly at the temple of the zombie before me.

My strike was true. The blade jarred my arm as it broke through the bone. The zombie fell to the side pulling my knife from my grasp. A new wail rose from the undead as my presence became known.

I reached out to pull my knife from the skull only to find it stuck fast. With no time to spare I let it go and ran, away from the car and in the opposite direction of Lily. The zombies faced with an easier meal to hand, followed as I had hoped. They came quickly, several actually managing to run. I cursed. That was not expected. I tried to increase my speed as I ran down the street, breath already starting to come in gasps, sweat breaking out. If I survived I resolved to definitely do more cardio.

At the end of the street was an intersection. The moans of the dead as they followed were already way too close for my liking. I cursed as I saw the street to the right filled with a number of zombies. The left had some but nowhere near as many. It irked that I was being forced by circumstances beyond my control to travel down paths not my choosing. I kept running.

An ache began to form in my left side warning me of the beginnings of a stitch. I ran past several zombies who gave chase as soon as they noticed me. I was fortunate they had all the reasoning ability of a corpse. If just one of them had decided to try and cut me off I would have been done for.

Ahead of me a large group of zombies stumbled and lurched onto the road I was running down. I was surrounded. I hoped it was happenstance and not some malevolent deity playing with me by having them surround me just as I had doubted their ability to do so. The zombies ahead, perhaps alerted by the moans of those behind me began to move in my direction.

The buildings around me contained smaller independent shops. These had smaller windows to display their wares and standard wooden doors with glass panelling rather than the automatic all glass doors of the larger chains. My options were limited as I dashed to the nearest door and tried to open it.

Despite a frantic attempt at both pushing and pulling, the first door was locked and refused to open. I moved as rapidly as I could to the second. My hand pressed to my side as I tried to relieve the pressure of my stitch. My lungs burned and my breath was laboured. I deeply regretted ever agreeing to help. The next door I tried was in a recessed entryway, it opened and I fell through slamming the door behind me and turning the small lock.

I lay on the hard linoleum covered floor as I waited for my breathing to return to a more measured rate. A loud thump caused the door to shake as the first zombie hit it, followed by a number of smaller thumps as its compatriots joined it. Their moans carried easily through the door. I watched as they pressed against the glass, the recess allowed only a couple to push against the door and the weight of the zombies behind ensured they couldn't raise their arms to hammer on the glass.

It was time to have a look around my safe haven. I hoped it would have a back door, if it didn't I could be in for a long and lonely wait for the zombies to break through.

The building I had found myself in was small. It was a single room with a small desk on which a cash register sat and a door lead to a back room. Numerous racks of clothing lined the walls and sat on the shop floor. So a clothes shop then. I had found refuge in a clothes shop. Whilst it would be pleasant to grab a change of clothing if time permitted, I did lament the fact that it was not a sports shop, a hunting store or any number of food retailers. All of which would provide things further along my list of needs than a change of clothes.

The zombies had spread out along the front of the building and were pressed up against the windows. Various disgusting fluids smeared the windows with each new creature that pushed up against the front of the building. I desperately needed a new weapon.

The clothing racks on the shop floor were cheap and shoddy material. I had no faith that the various parts would hold up to a serious attempt at a bludgeoning. Along the wall was a much more pleasing item. It was an eighteen inch chrome square tube in a general 'L' shape. It had seven chrome balls welded to one edge to allow for coat hangers to rest against and it was mounted on the wall with a small yet sturdy diamond shaped piece of metal at one end. Thin enough to cut through flesh if swung with enough force but not so thin it would immediately buckle at the first blow.

I stripped my new weapon of coat hangers as I dumped the clothes unceremoniously on the floor. It was attached to the wall by two small screws directly into the plaster. It took only a small amount of force to wrench it free of the wall. Happily armed with a weapon I went to check the back room. If I were lucky it would have a way out of this place.

My luck ran true to form. The back room held just a few boxes of clothing and some stairs leading to the second floor. The sound of glass breaking and renewed moans decided my next course of action. I pulled over a stack of boxes in front of the entranceway in hopes of delaying my gruesome pursuers and cautiously proceeded up the stairs.

The stairwell was narrow and dark, it changed course abruptly half way along its length. I was forced to tentatively peer around the corner before continuing to the top and a closed door. This door bore no lock and it was possible that the room beyond held the living quarters of the shop owner. I pressed my ear to the door and knocked.

Some muffled sounds were all I heard, perhaps an indication of an occupant; but no proof to say whether living or dead. I braced myself as best I could. Weapon raised above me ready to strike down, I opened the door.

Inside were the living quarters as suspected and devoid of life, living or dead. Before me was a simple living room with an open kitchen and two closed doors. The living room held a large sofa and an easy chair, both facing an old large TV. A mirror and a clock hung on the wall. It was a simple and plain room, somewhere to pass the time and not somewhere to live. The moans of the undead were becoming louder and sounded as though they came from the bottom of the stairs.

Once again the sofa formed the beginnings of a barricade. I slammed shut the door and manoeuvred the sofa up against it. I then picked up the chair and put that on top, followed by the heavy TV. It wasn't ideal but it would hold them off, I hoped.

I cast my eyes over the tiny kitchen area. It held very little in the way of useable items but in one of the drawers, I found several kitchen knives. Large flat blades with sharp edges, I placed two firmly beneath the door to the stairwell to act as doorstops. Just in time as the first zombie reached the door and attempted to break through.

The door now secure, I rooted through the kitchen looking for food. The fridge held some cheese and bread, along with lettuce and a few small tomatoes. I didn't bother making a sandwich. I just ate it all as quickly as I could after I made sure that I had scrubbed my hands free of the zombie juices first at the sink. A bottle of milk finished off my meal after a brief sniff to tell if it was safe.

A thump from behind one of the closed doors reminded me that I needed to clear the back rooms. I picked up my weapon and approached the first door which swung inwards to reveal an empty bathroom that consisted of a sink, toilet and shower. No place for a zombie to hide. I moved to the next.

As my hand touched the door handle a thump came once more from within. My mouth was suddenly dry and my pulse started to race. I took a firm grip on the handle, turned it and threw open the door.

The bedroom was taken up almost entirely by a large bed crammed against the far wall. On the opposite side of the room were a chest of drawers and wardrobe. On the bed a naked man lay spread-eagled amongst the sheets. Blood pooled on the bed and speckled the walls, furniture and even the ceiling. A fully clothed and very much dead woman knelt on the bed beside him. Her long blonde hair reddened at the ends as she bent over the ravaged flesh of his stomach, feeding. Blood and gore covered her face and chest. Her arms were caked a glistening crimson to her elbows.

With the door open the smell rushed out and I retched, the sound alerted the zombie to my presence. Her gaze caught mine and we stared at each other for what seemed to be an eternity. She opened wide her mouth and shrieked as she scrambled across the bed to reach me.

My arm dropped, weapon striking her with all the force I could muster. She collapsed to the floor as I struck her twice more to ensure that she would not rise again. My chest heaved and my hand ached from gripping so tightly to the metal of my weapon that was now bedecked with her blood, skin and hair. She had been fresh enough that I bore more than a little of her blood. If my barricade held then it would be time for a shower. First though I had to do one more thing. I walked slowly alongside the bed until I was within reach of the naked man's head. I struck once, twice then once again at his temple before dropping my weapon.

A small window was set into the wall above the bed, curtains closed. I played out what must have happened in my head. The owner asleep here in his room, his partner or staff member had opened the shop and managed to get herself somehow infected before heading back upstairs to clean the wound. She no doubt turned into one of the undead and attacked the man as he lay in his bed, perhaps knocking closed the door and trapping herself in the room.

Fortunate for me at least as it left the shop door unlocked just when I needed it. I opened the curtains letting in the morning sunlight to bathe the grisly scene. The window had a locking mechanism that only allowed it to open a little. It was enough to see that it was set above the front of the shop. Directly below I could see the street I had run down so short a time ago and a dozen zombies who had not yet managed to clamber through into the shop. In short there was no way out. I had trapped myself.

I left the bedroom and closed the door behind me as I leaned back against the wall. The exertions of this morning had taken their toll. I slowly let myself slide down until I was sat against the wall facing the front entrance. Two dead zombies behind me with an unknown number of hungry undead beyond the door and I was covered liberally in blood with no way out. I was trapped. I lowered my head and waited for the zombies to break through the front door.

Chapter 6

If Lily had done as she was supposed to, she would be waiting for me with Brian and whoever she had managed to rescue just a few streets away. I couldn't help but wonder how long she would wait for me to arrive before giving me up for dead. If the roles were reversed and if I were the one waiting, it wouldn't be long.

The noise the zombies made as they tried to enter this small apartment had begun to grate. From where I sat against the wall I could see the door shake as the mindless things tried to batter their way through. It hadn't taken long for despair at my situation to turn into boredom. I could always remove the barricade and try and fight my way out. That at least would provide a little excitement. It would be better than waiting anyway.

A fight to the death was much more deserving of a more formidable weapon than a clothes rack. I made my way around the living space searching for something to use. In the bedroom I found a cell phone, though having no numbers to call it would be little use. I did try the emergency services but whenever I dialled the number it was busy. I put the phone into my pocket anyway. It may come in useful later and my own phone had been forgotten when I left my home yesterday.

Beneath the sink I found a rusted toolbox containing no less than three screwdrivers, a pair of pliers and a claw headed hammer. I left the pliers and managed to place the three screwdrivers into my jacket pocket. I did have to pierce the material to make them fit but my gore covered clothing was ruined anyway. The hammer I kept to hand, it would be a handy weapon to help bludgeon my way to freedom.

I was taking one final look around the kitchen before I left when I noticed it. A ceiling hatch. It was set high in one corner above some cabinets. It was small and I may struggle to get through but it was something. It was perhaps more of a chance at survival than trying to fight my way free.

With a chance of escape my mood lightened and I went back into the bedroom. I searched through the cabinet and drawers. I put some socks, a couple of plain t-shirts and some shorts that looked like they might fit me into a black backpack that I found at the bottom of the cupboard. Then back to the kitchen where I added as much food as I could without over filling it.

To reach the hatch I had to climb onto the countertop and try to hold myself steady with one hand on the top cupboard as I reached across and pushed open the hatch. With the hatch open I could swing the backpack through, before grabbing onto the rough wooden ledge risking splinters. I stepped off of the countertop and swung free for a moment before heaving myself up and through the hole into the attic with trembling arms.

Within the attic all was darkness, the weak light coming through the ceiling hatch giving scant illumination. I pulled the dead man's phone from my pocket and switched it on. The light from the screen would serve as torch, it provided just enough to allow me to move around the attic space and see that it was empty.

As attics go it was fairly standard. A brick wall stood firm on either side of me, preventing access into the roof compartments of the neighbouring shops. Thick wooden beams ran from one wall to the next with thick insulation material filling the gaps between. The roof rose to a peak allowing me to stand fully upright only in the centre of the room.

Between the wooden joists that rose to the peak I could see the roof felt and timber laths that the slate tiles of the roof sat upon. The claw hammer proved invaluable as it ripped aside felt and thin lath with ease. The slate tiles were nailed in place and required some work with the hammer before I had broken enough to make a sizeable hole in the roof.

Dust filled the air and coated my clothes, sticking to the blood and various other fluids that hadn't yet dried fully. I looked a mess and would have dearly loved a shower. The light rain falling through the newly made hole in the roof wouldn't do much. I cautiously poked my head through the hole. The roof was thankfully zombie free. I grabbed my backpack and pulled myself through.

The tiles were slick with fresh fallen rain and I could see that the edge of the roof ended abruptly. No stone lip to prevent my falling on the zombies milling below. I very carefully pulled myself up the roof until I could sit on the ridge tile that capped the peak. The view was impressive.

Smoke wreathed the town. From my vantage point I could see much of the town centre. Peaked slate tile roofs atop two story buildings of stone, would give way abruptly to newer more imposing buildings of concrete and brick. It was easy to see how the town had changed as newer and more modern buildings were built.

Few cars were moving along the streets I could see, though each seemed to have a number of shambling figures. Around a few store fronts zombies would gather peering within.

They seemed able to tell which buildings had people hiding within. Perhaps they could smell the scared people or hear them. They could even have another sense for all I knew. One thing was obvious, they were hungry and they wouldn't stop until they got their prey.

The silence that had settled over the town was broken occasionally by the pop pop pop of gunshots in the distance. The police or the military were in town and fighting back. As loathe as I were to put myself into the hands of the forces of law and order, it had become clear that my initial thoughts that I would need to be a part of a group to be able to survive this were on the mark.

The park where I was supposed to have met Lily and the others was not visible from my current vantage point, but I could at least tell the general direction in which the street lay. Travelling across the rooftop would get me as far as the end of this block of buildings but I would still need some way down. Preferably a way that would allow me to slip quietly past the undead.

I made my way across the rain dampened rooftop. Backpack of supplies firmly strapped to my back and hammer in my hand. I was better supplied than I had been at the start of the day, so all was not a total loss. I reached the last building in the row and looked down from the edge.

The rain heavy clouds had by now completely covered the sky. Large droplets of water had begun to fall with an increased ferocity as though the very sky above wished to wash away the horrors that were taking place in the town below with this alley as a focal point for the weather gods' ferocity.

The alley between my perch and the building opposite was awash with blood. Pieces of meat that had once been human were scattered along the length. A horde of undead feasted on the remains. Whoever had been caught in this alley had encountered an unpleasant end. I cursed my misfortune. No safe way down would be found here.

A sheer drop was all I could see at either the front or back of the shops in this row. The main street at the other end held no way down and an alleyway full of zombies below me ensured I was running out of options. The roof of the building across the alley was flat and seemed to be my only choice. I just had to jump a six foot gap in the rain with zombies beneath me.

The rain wasn't letting up. Waiting would just make things harder. I pulled off the backpack and threw it along with the hammer across to the roof opposite. I backed across my roof half a dozen paces. The ridge tile that I had been walking upon was rounded and provided precarious footing at best.

Taking a deep breath I ran, arms pumping straight towards the edge of the roof. As my foot landed on the last ridge tile it slipped. Off balance I pushed down and threw myself forward across the gap, arms stretched out before me. I slammed into the side of the building, barely managing to grasp tight to the ledge that ran along the roof. Pain shot outwards from my chest along with all the air in my lungs.

My hands were locked tight to the ledge as I hung above the alley desperately sucking in air. I managed to haul myself up and over the ledge and onto the roof with arms that trembled from the exertion. I collapsed onto my back on the roof as the rain fell around me. That had been entirely too close.

The pain above my ribs wasn't receding. I placed a hand under my jacket and found that one of the screwdrivers I had placed in the inside pocket of my jacket had cut deeply into my flesh when I hit the side of the building. Blood was flowing freely.

My jacket and t-shirt were removed carefully as I made sure to hold the material away from the open wound. With the amount of zombie blood they were covered with, I dare not risk any chance of infection. I retrieved the back pack and removed one of the clean t-shirts I had looted from the flat. With a little effort I was able to rip the cloth and fashion some rudimentary bandages. Hardly ideal but it was certainly better than walking around with an open wound.

I pulled the second t-shirt on and slipped my arms into the straps of the backpack wincing as the movement pulled the edges of my wound. I picked up the hammer and considered the options I had for getting back down to the ground. The side facing the alleyway held no way out. The front of the building held just a straight drop down onto the zombie infested street all along its length. The building I stood upon ended against a four story office block. I was left with only the rear of the structure. Damp, aching and feeling dejected I headed across the roof.

A fire escape led down to the ground from a door set just below the roof, thankfully far from the zombie filled alleyway I had just tried to jump. The metal stairs of the fire escape led into a courtyard that trucks would use to unload deliveries for the stores that surrounded it. I lowered myself from the roof and dropped the remaining few feet onto the sturdy metal landing.

The door was closed with no way of opening it from the outside so I quietly made my way down the stairs and crossed the courtyard to the gap between the buildings that the trucks would drive through. Checking for the dead, moving or otherwise I made my way around the buildings and headed towards the meeting place.

Rain seemed to confuse the zombies. While the slow walk towards where I hoped to meet Lily was in no way safe, it seemed easier to remain undetected. If I kept out of their direct line of sight and didn't move too close, I could pass them by. I hid behind parked or abandoned cars and in recessed doorways, keeping low and creeping slowly as I did my best to watch all around me.

At one point I encountered a large group moving down the street towards me. Their numbers spread from one side of the street to the other. With no way of fighting such a group I was forced to drop to the ground and crawl beneath a van. I had a tense wait as I lay on the tarmac of the road and counted the seconds as the group moved past. My head turning first one way and then another trying to see every direction at once, mouth dry and my heart beat rising. My stomach lurched with every stumbling pair of feet that passed too close to where I was hidden.

When I finally crawled from beneath the van the street was empty. The zombies all gathered along in the wake of the large group that had passed, swelling its ranks. It freed me to move swiftly to the end of the street and into the next.

I was cold and wet by the time I reached the meeting place, a small park that sat in the centre of the town. It was a place for office workers to eat their lunches away from their desks, for families to take a break from shopping where the children could run around on the grass chasing pigeons. It was a place full of life and noise. Now it was empty, Lily and the rest of the little group I had risked my life to save were nowhere to be seen.

Chapter 7

The park had always been a pleasant place to sit and watch the world go by. I had first noticed no less than three of my victims whilst sat watching the people as they sat and talked or quietly ate. The green grass had always been well tended, whilst the trees and bushes that bordered the park were kept neat and orderly.

Slumped on a bench in the park cold, wet and very much alone as I stared into space; I couldn't feel any of that previous pleasure. The heavy rain that fell from the dark grey sky above suited my mood. Lily had abandoned me. I felt more than a little betrayed and used.

In the end it was the ache from the deep gash in my side that forced me to get up off the bench. I wanted some pain killers and an actual bandage. If I was forced to do this alone then so be it. I worked best alone I told myself and tried to sound convincing. My first task would be to get out of the town centre and find somewhere safe to get some rest. I just had no idea where.

Lily had said the football stadium was going to be used to gather refugees so I could always go there, though that was likely her destination and I was in no mood to encounter her. I recalled that on the edge of the town were some blocks of flats. I could get somewhere off the ground floor and barricade myself in one of them and at least have a proper shower and some decent rest before deciding what to do. Mind made up I set off. Distracted by the ache in my side and dwelling on my feelings of betrayal, I didn't see the zombie until I was almost on top of him.

Startled from my reverie I stumbled back. The dead man lurched at me. He was missing an eye along with a large part of his face. Congealed blood stained his shirt and discoloured his suit. He moaned as he tried to grab me, swollen tongue protruding grotesquely from his mouth. I sidestepped his clumsy movements and swung the hammer against his head.

My first swing didn't manage to hit full on and just glanced off of his skull. The blow didn't faze him and he was on me. His grip was like iron and I struggled to dislodge him as I used all of my strength just to keep him at bay. His ruined face was all I could see as he tried to sink his teeth into my exposed flesh.

He was pulling himself closer as we struggled. With no room to swing I couldn't get enough force to break his skull. As I became increasingly desperate I reversed the hammer and hooked the clawed side of the head into his ruined socket. I pulled on the hammers handle and was rewarded with a loud crack as bone was fractured.

I kicked out and stopped pulling away. The combination of the zombie pulling me as his leg was kicked out beneath him caused him to lose balance and fall back. I landed on top of him and pushed my elbow against his throat, pinning his head down. I swung my hammer at his weakened skull again and again until he stopped moving.

Another zombie had been defeated. It had not been elegant and I was once more spattered with blood and bits of brain, but I had beaten it. I smiled and wanted to laugh. My dark mood had dissipated, replaced by a sense of satisfaction and general pleasant feeling.

With a renewed sense of optimism I set off once again for the block of flats. The journey didn't take long, with the outskirts of the town being fairly quiet. Few undead wandered the streets and the ones I did see were easily avoided. The rain was starting to let up by the time I reached the flats and the few zombies I had encountered were becoming more active.

I entered the block of flats slowly. The lock at the main entrance was broken so the door swung inwards easily. The ground floor flats were silent, doors closed and the few I tried were locked. I tried knocking on some of the doors and received no response. An elevator stood at the end of the hall and beside it a door that led to a stairwell. I decided it would be safer to take the stairs.

The first floor was just as quiet. A plain hallway that ended with a window set into a wall. A trail of blood led from the open door of the nearest flat and led towards the elevator. This floor had four doors; two on either side of the hallway three of them were closed and locked. I listened closely with my ear pressed up against the doors, first one and then another as I tried to determine if the flats were occupied. I couldn't hear anything.

A glance through the open door had revealed a scene of carnage. Blood splashed the walls and floor, furniture was overturned and the only light came from the flickering TV screen. I couldn't hear anything moving within but didn't want to risk entering. I really wasn't feeling up to another fight to the death.

None of the closed doors were unlocked so I chose one that was on the opposite side to the main entrance on the floor below. The block of flats was maintained by the local council as low income housing. As a result the doors and the locks were cheap. A few blows with the hammer over the lock easily splintered the wood and the door fell open. The obvious problem it created was that I would need yet another barricade if I wanted to have any sort of safety.

The flat I had chosen was dingy. Dust covered the surfaces and the window didn't look as though it had ever been cleaned. Worn carpet covered the floor and a single three seater couch sat in the centre of the room, the fabric fraying and greasy to the touch. A few family pictures of children sat in frames on the mantel. A TV sat in the corner on its stand, remote carelessly left on the floor by the couch.

I considered for a moment choosing another flat, but finally decided that with the world gone to hell I had better get used to less than pleasant living conditions. I checked the rest of the flat for anyone living or dead. A small kitchen, bathroom and bedroom completed the living space and were all empty.

The fridge contained little of worth so I unplugged it and dragged it over to the door. It blocked the door from opening and would be difficult to move from outside the flat. I picked up a shot glass from a kitchen shelf and placed it inside a cup before balancing it on the edge of the fridge. If anyone tried to open the door it would rock the fridge and knock off the cup and glass making plenty of noise. I would have plenty of warning of someone entering.

I spent the next hour looking through the cupboards and drawers. I found a small amount of food that I considered edible and nutritious. Some thankfully clean towels and a small first aid kit that didn't hold much but did have some antiseptic, gauze and tape.

A long hot shower washed away many of my aches. I stood under the hot water and scrubbed away the blood and muck that I had acquired since Lily first knocked on my door. When I was done with the shower I couldn't bear to touch my soiled clothing and so left them on the bathroom floor. I dried myself with the towel before wrapping it around my waist and heading into the living room to sit on the couch.

I dosed my wound liberally in antiseptic wincing at the stinging, before taping the gauze over the cut. I leaned back on the couch and turned on the TV. I flipped through the channels until I found a news station and ate my fill as I caught up on the news.

The news presenters were panicked. It wasn't easy to pick up but if you watched closely you could see that the way they held themselves rigid, keeping a tight control over themselves and their movements. The twitch of an eye or mouth in response to a fresh piece of information passed to them. They had a general air of fear that I was all too familiar with from my own victims. They were giving out bad news and were holding back worse.

Throughout the rest of the day and long into the night I watched. Image after image would flash by on the screen. Stills captured from CCTV or uploaded from someone's phone. Images of the dead attacking, ripping and rending flesh. The terrified faces of the people being killed preserved for us to see.

Video clips would play of entire cities on the move. A terrified populace fleeing in their cars, packed full of all those precious items they held so dear. The same items soon abandoned as the roads became one endless traffic jam and beyond them the dead, following tirelessly desperate to feed.

The scenes were repeated endlessly. The largest cities were the first to fall. Too many people packed together with nowhere to run. Entire city blocks became charnel houses, the streets were red rivers of blood and throughout it all one thing remained the same. If the dead killed you, you would rise. Born anew as a zombie ready to follow your undead brethren and feast on the living.

Across the world the scenes were repeated. Ships at sea were left to float offshore, no safe harbour to sail into. Beleaguered armies were fighting and falling. The living, were fighting a losing war. Every man, woman or child who died would become another zombie to kill.

Sometime around three in the morning the news reported that China had set off a nuclear device over one of their southern cities. More bombs fell through the night as the leaders of that nation tried desperately to halt the tide. It was a futile effort. If only half their population turned, they would still have more than five hundred million zombies. Our world was paying a harsh price for having a population of more than seven billion.

I tried to get a few hours sleep in the flats tiny bedroom after I first pushed a chest of drawers across the bedroom door, it was better to be safe than sorry. Even so my sleep was still fitful. By 7 o'clock I had given up on sleep and was sat back on the couch eating some dry cereal and watching the TV.

The rest of the day followed the same pattern. Eat and drink and watch TV. Occasionally during a period of the news presenters repeating the same things, I would stand at the window and look out at the world beyond.

It was quiet out on the streets. A few cars went past and one coach packed full of people and their belongings headed towards the motorway. I didn't think they would get far. The zombies were growing in number. Groups both large and small moved through the town, their bodies ranging from the barely touched to the falling apart at the seams.

At one point I did see a helicopter fly over the town. It looked military and was headed north. No planes seemed to be flying anymore. Not long after the helicopter flew over a convoy of army trucks drove through the town. I had no idea where they were going but I heard no more sounds of gunfire afterwards.

I spent a second night in the flat. I told myself it was so that I could rest though in truth I was feeling lost and unable to decide on a course of action. Since Lily knocked on my door I had been reacting. My decision to go to a library to gather much needed knowledge had ended badly, though I was still convinced I would need to go back at some point.

Over the years I had grown used to working alone. It had never bothered me that I had few friends and no close family. I was fine moving through life dependent on no one but myself. At the start of this whole apocalypse though, my first instinct had been that I would need to be part of a group to survive. That initial group I had been trying to form had abandoned me. Sleep eluded me once more.

The morning was cold and a light rain was falling. I took a hot shower and finished the last of the food I had found in the flats kitchen before dressing for the first time in days. I grabbed my backpack and hammer before moving the fridge away from the door. Hiding away unable to make a decision was no way to live. It was time to make a choice and right or wrong I would live or die by it.

Cautiously I peeked around the door. All was quiet in the hallway so I headed for the stairs, keeping to the wall opposite the door that had been open when I arrived. The stairwell was empty and I left the block of flats without incident. It seemed prudent to keep away from the main roads so I set off walking around the side of the flats and across the nearby car park.

Before long I had reached my destination. The canal that ran past the town centre and out across the country. It should be ideal. I could follow the canal out of town and avoid the roads and motorways that would be likely impassable with abandoned vehicles and zombies.

The walk was almost pleasant. For a time I could hear birds singing their songs in the trees. I hadn't seen any birds or any animal in fact, whilst in the town centre. I wondered if that were due to the infection that created the zombies or the zombies themselves. Yet another question to add to the growing list that would need answering at some point in the future.

An hour later I came upon a brightly painted canal boat that floated serenely just beyond the path, a rope attached to either end of the boat connected to a mooring pin that had been hammered into the ground. I approached cautiously.

As I neared the back of the boat a door opened and a man stepped out holding a black double barrelled shotgun. He looked to be middle aged, short greying hair and a neat beard covered a wide face. He had dark coloured jeans and a yellow windbreaker. The shotgun was definitely pointed towards me.

"What do you want?" he said, voice deep and confident. I cast away any doubt that he would use the gun if he needed to. I raised my hands to show I meant no harm.

"Just passing by my friend." I said with what I hoped to be a nice soothing tone.

"Aye, you do just that." He gestured with the rifle, the smallest of jerks to the side to indicate I should move on. I could see movement behind him within in the boat.

"Before I go, are you able to tell me what the conditions are like back there" I said pointing along the canal in the direction I happened to be going and where unless he had turned his boat around, he had come from.

"Not good" he said after a moments thought. "These bloody dead men are walking around everywhere biting folk."

"Where have you come from?"

"Sheffield. It was bad back there. We barely got out" he said with a nod of his head towards the dark interior of the boat. "We've had people try to steal our boat twice already, and been attacked by one of those things once."

"That's terrible to hear. These are not good times." I said with as much false sincerity as I could muster. Perhaps these people would look fondly on someone willing to join them and help protect their boat.

"Aye it certainly is." He agreed, lowering the rifle so that it wasn't pointed so obviously towards me. I took that as a good sign. "I still can't believe what's happening, one of those bloody things even bit my Evie before I shot the bugger."

"I am sorry to hear that. Is she ok?" Would a bite that didn't cause death infect someone? I suspected it might and this man obviously didn't.

"She was a bit upset so she's having a lie down. I had to use half a bottle of antiseptic. Dirty things. No idea what germs they have." He said.

"Well sir it has been a pleasure to meet you and I wish you well but I think I shall continue along my way." I said with as much fake cheer as I could.

The shotgun bearing man said a brief farewell and watched as I walked away from the boat, rifle still held at the ready. I soon turned a bend and the boat was lost to sight. I sat down on the path and waited.

Two hours later the sounds of panicked shouting followed by the thunderous roar of a shotgun as it fired echoed along the canal bank. I waited a few more minutes and then crept slowly around the bend so that I could see the boat.

All seemed quiet and ordinary, the boat sat still in the calm waters. Then the door at the back of the boat opened outwards and the man I had met staggered out. His shotgun was no longer with him and he looked distressed. Tears fell down his face and he clutched his arm, blood leaking from between his fingers. I had been right. This "Evie" must have turned and attacked him before he managed to shoot her.

Curiosity satisfied I returned to my journey. One of my questions had an answer. I had been right to avoid getting any zombie fluids in my wounds. It did raise yet more questions though. Did the length of time it took to turn change depend on how much of the infection you received or where the infection entered your system. That would be something to think about. I really hated not knowing.

I had no more encounters along the canal bank. It was quiet and fairly stress free all the way. Soon enough though I had reached the point where I would leave the canal. In the distance I could just make out the football stadium to the north east. Lights attached to the walls of the stadium were switched on and I could see movement at the entrances. It was time to re-join whatever remnants of civilisation remained, crammed into that large imposing edifice.

Chapter 8

The town's football stadium was a fairly new structure. Built in the early nineties, it could comfortably house twenty to twenty-five thousand people. It was enclosed on all four sides with large banks of seating surrounding the sports field in the centre. Attached to the east side was a gym complete with swimming pool and sauna. It jutted out from the side of the stadium adding little to the aesthetics.

Large car parks could be found at the north and south entrances, a road ran along the east side of the stadium linking the two. An impressive looking steel security fence surrounded the entire place with secure gates at the north and south entrances.

These gates had been augmented with a wall of sandbags and mounted machine guns. Armed soldiers walked the perimeter in pairs whilst land rovers bedecked in the green hues of the military, drove up and down the streets.

Within the barrier the tarmac that would hold hundreds of vehicles on game days, was buried beneath a sea of tents. Families huddled together, husbands and wives holding their children close. An air of desperation blanketed the area.

I walked towards the south gates, stopping and raising my arms whenever a land rover drove by. I barely rated a glance from the hard eyed men and women driving, being unarmed I imagine that they considered me little threat. I had already stashed the hammer in my backpack. Further along the road and more so before the gates, the ground was spotted with dark patches that looked to be blood and other unidentifiable substances. The whole area reeked of death.

The sentries dutifully ignored me once they realised I was a living breathing person and concentrated on their jobs. As I reached the gates one was pulled open and a soldier holding his rifle at the ready gestured me in.

The soldier bade me follow him as he walked along the fence to a large tent set away from the others. Several soldiers stood guard around it and I began to feel a little concern. My escort stopped at the entrance and gestured at me to continue. I stepped into the tent.

Within the tent all was quiet, it was easily tall enough to allow me to stand upright. Cloth partitions surrounded me. A pretty young lady in combat fatigues and a white coat came around the fabric wall to my left.

"Hi there. Welcome to our little hospital." She said with a smile. "You just arrived I take it?"

"Yes just minutes ago. What's going on?" I asked.

"Standard procedure I'm afraid. We need to make sure you are clear of infection before we let you into the general population." She smiled at me again; I suspected she was trying to put me at ease.

"Don't worry we have been checking all the new arrivals. We didn't actually expect any more. The roads are pretty bad out there." She chattered on as she led me back the behind the partition she had first stepped through.

The small space was empty but for a stern soldier holding a rifle. I began to sweat. "It's ok" she said noticing my concern "he is just here for our protection. If you aren't infected you will be fine."

"And if I am infected?" The soldier stood a little straighter and clutched his rifle tight as I said that. He didn't blink as he stared at me.

"If you have been bitten, or have an open wound and obvious signs of infection; this soldier will take you to a holding area. If you are still ok after twenty four hours you will be checked over and given the all clear to enter the camp. If you are infected you will turn and, well we wouldn't have much choice then would we." She said before adding, "You need to get undressed please."

Neither the medic nor the soldier showed any indication of allowing me privacy so I reluctantly dropped my backpack and started removing my clothes.

"What happened there?" asked the medic as I removed my t-shirt. The soldier had the rifle up and pointed directly at me. I stood as still as I could, doing my best to appear unthreatening.

"An accident a couple of days ago, I cut myself" I said, careful to stress that it was not recent. The medic pulled away the gauze, the tape doing its painful best to remain attached to my skin. She inspected the deep cut. Despite the antibacterial I had used, the skin around the wound looked red and inflamed.

"Ok. It's certainly not recent but it does look like you might have a standard infection. I can give you antibiotics to help combat it. Do you have any other wounds you need to tell me about?" she asked, as she looked towards the soldier and gave a small nod. He lowered the rifle again.

I told her that I had no others and explained that I had been hidden away for the last two days as I finished removing my clothes. The medic gave me a thorough and more than a little embarrassing inspection. Finally she gave the all clear and allowed me to dress once more. The soldier relaxed and I breathed a sigh of relief.

The medic led me back to the front and I was handed over to a soldier stationed outside the tent's entrance before she handed me a small bottle of pills retrieved from a pocket of her coat and scurried back to whatever she had been doing before I arrived. The soldier led me towards yet another tent set away from the main camp. This tent was a hive of activity, soldiers of all ranks bustled about their business.

The soldier left me with a portly man dressed in the now familiar military garb and seated behind a table just outside the tent. He identified himself as the quartermaster and filled me in on the basic camp rules. I would be given a blanket if I did not have one. The tents and sleeping bags had all been taken days before. I could sleep anywhere around the stadium that I could find space provided I was out of the way of the soldiers.

Food was in short supply with so many people, so meals were rationed and provided once a day. Water was still running but to get any I would likely have to queue. Inside the stadium and sports centre were toilet facilities but again the camp held far too many people, so temporary port-a-loos had been set up around the camps.

The camp rules were fairly simple. Any theft, fighting or rape and you would be kicked from the camp. The soldiers here were too few in number to do much more than guard the perimeter so they certainly had no capacity to care for prisoners. If you killed someone or interfered with the military operation you would be executed. That order had been given by the military high command with the backing of the government just days before.

If I obeyed the rules, I could spend my time as I pleased. If I wanted to leave and they could open the gates safely, then I was free to do so. If someone left though, it was unlikely they would be allowed back in. Too many chances someone would bring the infection back in with them. The quartermaster solemnly informed me that an incident just after the camp was set up had caused the deaths of fifteen people. The military would not be taking any more chances.

The atmosphere of the camp was overwhelming. Thousands of people crammed into one place with limited access to water, stank to high heaven. The noise was constant. People talking in low tones, arguments and swearing were commonplace. No laughter and no smiling faces, just an undercurrent of despair.

I spent the few hours that remained before it would become too dark to do much of anything, exploring my new home. I moved through the press of humanity, always keeping a wary eye out for somewhere to spend the night.

Within the stadium itself, thousands filled the seats. Anyone who cared to look would be unable to see the grass of the pitch due to the sheer number of people huddled together on it. The corridors and rooms that filled the stadium itself had become a home to the dirty masses. Children and adults alike wept for loved ones they had lost. As the day wore on, I couldn't help but become claustrophobic.

The stadium was too crowded for my taste. It would only need one person with the infection to turn. In the press of humanity I doubted anyone would even notice and then with no place to run, they would be sitting ducks.

Even though the nights were becoming colder as the days moved ever further away from summer, I decided to sleep outside. I chose a spot by the outer wall of the gym, away from the worst of the wind and most of the people and lay down. The area was quiet being so close to the fence that ended against the gym wall. That seemed to put people off which suited me well. My backpack served as a pillow and I wrapped myself in the blanket and fell asleep.

I was awakened before dawn by the pop pop of many guns firing. The sound seemed to come from the north. The firing continued for several minutes before silence fell once more. The zombies it seemed were approaching the camp.

Sleep would not return. I couldn't get comfortable and the cold was seeping into my very bones. I gave up and decided to have a look at what was happening at the north gate. I gathered up my few possessions and made my way around the stadium and through the camps.

By the time I had reached the gate, the soldiers were dragging away the last of the corpses. A few other curious civilians had gathered to watch. The majority though seemed unwilling to leave the warmth of their blankets or tents.

The soldiers had soon returned to their routine and I had grown bored of watching them. In truth I was bored with the whole camp already. I spent the rest of the day wandering aimlessly around the camp. Occasionally the monotony would be broken by a group of zombies approaching the camp. They were quickly despatched and it was not really that much fun to watch someone else shoot them. In the late afternoon I joined the long lines of people waiting for food and had a fairly unappetizing meal before settling down once more for the night in my corner by the gym.

I awoke the next day feeling out of sorts and irritable. I sat and leaned back against the stadium wall wrapped in my blanket, and stared morosely through the fence. Nothing moved on the road beyond. The gunfire was heard often and from several places throughout the day but I couldn't even rouse enough interest to go and watch the zombies as they were gunned down.

The boredom was becoming too much. I could feel no special desire to try and talk to anyone within the camp. They were all too fearful, too content to let the soldiers protect them as they hid here. I ran my hand across my chin. I needed a shave and a shower but could find no way to do either whilst in the camp. It was time to go. I had made a mistake coming to this place. It was not for the likes of me. I would be better suited taking my chances outside the camp, even if I was alone.

There would be no point in wasting any more time. I still had a little food hidden away in my backpack and whilst the soldiers had been cleaning out the nearby supermarkets for food to supply the people here, a great many houses would still contain items of use for someone who was not squeamish about removing the occupants whether living or dead.

I stood slowly and stretched. I had been sat in one place so long my muscles had stiffened. I pulled on the backpack and headed for the gates to the south. As I approached I couldn't miss the commotion. The soldiers had the gates shut tight and were gathered before them listening to one of the officers speak.

A crowd of worried people had gathered. I approached the nearest soldier and asked. "What's going on?"

"Zombies are coming. Lots of them." He said. "Looks like we are going to be having a rough time."

"Ah. I was actually headed out. Which way are they coming from so I can head in the opposite direction?"

The soldier looked at me and snorted. "You aren't going anywhere mate. Gates are shut and camps on lockdown."

"Even the north gate?"

"Yes. We have a shit ton of zombies headed this way. No one is going in or out. No point, nowhere to go." He said before he ran over to a group of soldiers by the medical tent.

It was typical of my luck of late. Decide to leave just as I became stuck in the camp. I felt a very real urge to scream and have a tantrum.

"Ryan?" A familiar voice called from somewhere close by. "Oh my God that is you!"

I turned just in time to see Lily running towards me. Arms stretched out as she embraced me. "We thought you were dead." She said through tears.

"What?" I said more than a little shocked by her sudden appearance.

Lily gazed up at me through tear filled eyes. "We waited for you and you didn't turn up. We thought you were dead." She said smiling. "What happened to you?"

I quickly filled her in on what had happened to me after we separated. I kept it short and left out a couple of things that may have upset her. When I had finished she just stood smiling at me. I was very aware of the fact that she was still holding on to me.

"I am so glad to see you. I was worried. Come on you have to meet Claire, she will want to see you." She said as she grabbed my hand and started to pull me through the growing crowd of worried onlookers.

"Who is Claire?" I asked.

Lily looked back at me, smile still fixed in place. "Claire was in the car with her daughter. She will be so happy to know you are alive so she can thank you."

She seemed genuinely happy to see me, so I didn't protest too much as she led me through the crowd and into the stadium. My mood had lightened considerably and the prospect of being stuck within the camp didn't seem so terrible.

As I followed Lily my thoughts turned back to the approaching zombies and the worry I had sensed in the soldier. The stadium wouldn't be able to hold out against any group of zombies large enough to require them to lockdown both gates. It would be just a matter of time before they managed to get in. I would need to find a way out and as I held onto Lily's hand, her flesh warm and not unpleasant, I decided that I would need to get her out too.

Chapter 9

Claire was a petite lady in her mid thirties. Mousey blond hair cut in a tight bob. She wore glasses, too much lipstick and eye shadow with tight fitting jeans, trainers and a t-shirt that depicted some band from the nineties. She had the bubbliest personality of anyone I had ever known and she hugged me for an uncomfortable amount of time. Her daughter Maggie was eight and shy. I was generally fine with that, being the quiet type myself. When Claire had finally released me I was the recipient of a hug from Maggie.

I had never been a fan of touching other people in general. I tolerated it when it was necessary and of course during sex, but as a general rule a hand shake was often too much contact. To be hugged and touched by so many people at once was entirely uncomfortable.

Claire, Maggie and Lily had all set up camp inside the stadium. They had arrived early enough to receive a sleeping bag for Maggie and blankets for themselves. They had made a nest of sorts at the top of one of the stands. With just enough space between the top row of seats and the wall, it was snug but helped them share body heat at night. It also gave them some added security.

Lily and Claire alternated talking as they filled me in on what had happened since we had parted. It seemed that Claire, her boyfriend Pete and her daughter Maggie had been fleeing the town. Their intention had been to meet her parents at their lodge in the Lake District some hundred miles or so away.

Driving through the town the front driver side tyre had blown. Pete had managed to pull into the side street before getting out of the car to assess the damage. This had happened early enough in the crisis that the undead weren't swarming everywhere, but not nearly early enough as one had attacked Pete as he bent about his task.

Claire had been forced to sit in the car, shielding Maggie as best she could as Pete died beside her door. She had locked all the doors and waited for the zombie to move on. Before long though others, perhaps smelling the fresh spilled blood had joined the first. Claire had hugged her daughter to her breast and prayed they wouldn't be noticed.

When Pete rose beside the door, his almost unrecognisable face peering through the window it had been too much. Claire cried out and Maggie had caught a glimpse out of the window. It was her scream we had heard that day that had caught our attention.

Lily took over the tale then. Explaining that after I had led the zombies away, she and Brian approached the car to find Claire and Maggie in tears and almost hysterical. With the very real fear that more of the undead would turn up at any moment, they had coaxed Claire and her daughter from the car. They gathered a few of their belongings and set off down the street in the opposite direction from where I had run. Lily had the foresight to try and retrieve my knife. After finding it stuck fast in the skull of the zombie I had killed she gave up and took the tyre iron that had been dropped by Pete when he was attacked.

They had been fortunate that their walk along the streets was generally uneventful. One moment of danger came when a zombie staggered through a doorway as they passed. It lunged at Brian who, in a panic to escape its grasp had carelessly knocked Maggie into its path. Lily's face flushed as she said this, her hands clenched into fists. Claire pulled her daughter close. I felt more than a little anger myself. I should have killed Brian when I had first met him.

Brian may have failed, but Lily had responded quickly. With the life of a child in danger she had leaped at the zombie, swinging the tyre iron for all she was worth. She managed to bludgeon the zombie before it hurt Maggie. She had more than a few choices words to say to Brian after that.

By the time they arrived at the park they were all tired and scared. Lily assured me that they waited as long as they could but eventually Brian managed to convince them that I must have died. A group of undead approaching the park where they waited was the decider. They had to go.

I waved off Lily's apologies here and she continued her story. They had left the park and were not far from the same block of flats I had found respite in when a military convoy had passed. The soldiers quickly had them in the back of a truck with some other refugees and brought them here.

When they were through the gate, Lily had made it clear that she had no interest in Brian sticking with them. Claire and Maggie eager for any familiar face had stayed with her. I asked if they had seen Brian since then and Lily shook her head. Claire told me that she thought she had seen him in the corridors beneath the north stands, though she couldn't be certain. I smiled at her and changed the subject, though Lily gave me a long look.

The fact that Brian was somewhere in here caused a need within me. I wanted to finish what I had started days before when I stabbed him in the leg. The fact that I would need to hunt him as the zombies assaulted the gates and privacy seemed to be a thing of the past in this overcrowded place just added extra appeal.

At Lily's prompt I told Claire what had happened after I ran away followed by the zombies. She was an appreciative audience, staring rapt as I recounted the peril. When I finished with Lily finding me by chance here, Claire reached over and engulfed me in another hug.

"Thank you." She said quietly.

"Think nothing of it." I said as I awkwardly patted her back. "The danger isn't over for us. We need to leave here."

"Why? The soldiers are keeping us safe." Claire said as she sat back down beside her daughter.

I explained what the soldier had told me and added, "I really don't think this place will be safe for long."

Lily looked thoughtful and Claire worried. "I am going to have a look around, see if I can find a way out for us. Perhaps we can make our way to your parents." I said as I stood.

Claire seemed to like that idea and nodded her agreement. As I walked away Lily followed and grabbed hold of my arm, speaking low to avoid being overheard. "I know what you are thinking." She said.

"Oh?"

"He is a prick but you can't just kill him."

"I have no intention of killing anyone. I am just going to look for a way out." I lied.

Lily glared at me. "That's bull and you know it. Do not lie to me Ryan." Her hand tightened on my arm. "I like you. You have saved my life more than once and I am more than happy that you are alive and here with us now."

"But?"

"But, I can't be a party to you killing innocent people. I just can't. I know that you have killed people before and I owe you enough not to tell anyone, but if you stay with us you have to stop."

"I can't help who I am Lily. Perhaps it would be better for us to part now." I couldn't help the lurch my stomach gave at the thought. In my life I had few friends and none had ever known the real me. Lily did know me and wasn't running for the hills. I really didn't want to lose her again.

Long seconds passed as Lily, head tilted to the side and lips pressed tightly together considered my words. Finally she spoke. "I think we would do better together. I don't think anyone will survive alone out there." She sighed. "If we stay together though we will need some rules."

"Such as?"

"You can't hurt children." She said.

"That is one thing I will agree to unconditionally. I have no interest in that." I said with a more genuine smile.

"If you have to kill someone, restrict yourself to those that deserve it. God knows they're enough of those around these days." Lily said. "An apocalypse seems to bring the worst out in people."

I had to think about that. On the one hand I had to agree that we would doubtless meet many people who would mean us harm as society crumbled. On the other hand though, it would cross Brian off the list. Reluctantly I agreed.

"Good. So no Brian, and no lying to me. Ever." Lily said firmly.

"Yes fine, I won't kill Brian." I felt a little sorrow at that but it would pass no doubt.

"Ok. What do you need me to do?"

"Huh?"

"To get ready to leave dummy," she said with a smile. "You don't have to do everything yourself."

"Oh. Of course. I will look for a way out. You could gather up any food, blankets and perhaps see if you can scrounge a few medical supplies." I said.

Lily nodded and we agreed to meet back at her rest spot before dark. I walked away with a lighter step. The rules weren't ideal for me at all, but I could already see loopholes big enough to drive a truck through. I would stick to the letter of the terms. I hummed an old pop tune as I looked for a way out of the mess we seemed to be in.

I stepped out of the south entrance to the sound of gunfire and screaming. The zombies had arrived. Beyond the fence hundreds if not thousands of the undead pushed forward, determined to reach the living.

The soldiers stood in a line firing between the bars of the steel security fence. The land rovers I had previously seen patrolling along the roads were parked behind the gates. They were an extra barrier to help prevent the opening of the gates. Two soldiers stood atop each, firing down into the crowd of the walking dead. Civilians were streaming towards the north around the side of the stadium in a panic.

The zombies were bunching up against the gates and slowly moving outwards along the fence. From where I stood I couldn't see how many were coming this way but the numbers weren't thinning out.

All too soon the zombies stopped falling when shot. Too many were pushing against them from behind. The soldiers were rapidly reaching the point where they were just wasting bullets. Officers were screaming orders at their troops and fear was writ on every face. They knew they couldn't hold. I turned and ran back inside as the sounds of gunfire drifted down from the north.

I had to push my way through crowds of scared people. Panic was spreading like a wave through the stadium. Children cried and adults screamed at each other, as they begged for help or salvation.

Lily was already with Claire and Maggie by the time I arrived sporting several fresh bruises from the fight through the crowd. They were gathering together their small belongings, remarkably calm compared to the people around us.

"We have to go now." I shouted to be heard above the din.

"Where to?" asked Claire.

That was exactly the question I had been asking myself as I worked my way through the crowd. An answer had come slowly. "We need to head towards the gym." I said.

Lily just nodded and picked up her final belongings from the ground. She had enough faith in me to not question. Claire didn't know me well enough, but trusted Lily. Maggie had no choice. I smiled at her and waggled my eyebrows. She just looked down and took Claire's hand.

I led the way down through the stand and into the corridor beneath. It was hard work, people were moving in every direction desperately looking for a place of safety. Within the corridors we couldn't hear the shooting from the gates above the noise. We had no idea if the zombies had broken through or not. We reached the main entrance to the gym with little more than a few new bruises. I held the door and urged the others through.

Inside the gym all was calmer. The panic hadn't seemed to spread within yet. The doors had opened to a reception area. Motivational posters and flyers covered the walls. Makeshift beds covered the floor along with the detritus of human habitation. Men and women of all ages sat on the floor. Some speaking quietly together, others sat with eyes closed trying to get whatever rest they could.

We had barely made it through the doors when the screaming started behind us. Faint at first, it soon grew in volume the sound reverberating from the corridor walls. Beyond the entrance people were moving faster, they pushed against each other. I saw a man push aside a woman carrying a small child. She fell to the ground and was lost beneath the feet of the panicked masses.

"Close the doors and barricade them if you want to have any chance to survive!" I yelled as I pulled Lily through the doors to the gym.

A young man beside the entrance had been looking out at the crowd moving down the corridor. He called after me. "What's going on?"

"They're inside the building." I replied. His face lost all colour and he reached for the door. Cries of dismay rose around us. Two more men rose from their seats and moved to help with the door.

"What about the people outside?" asked one middle aged woman from where she sat.

"What about them? We can't fit everyone in here." A balding man in what would have once been an expensive suit responded. More voices yelled out questions and declarations. We left them to it and let the gym doors close behind us.

We found ourselves in a large room. The walls were covered floor to ceiling in mirrors. TVs hung from the roof silent and dark. The various pieces of gym equipment that were not firmly attached to the floor had been pushed against the far wall to make room for people to sleep. A great many people filled the room. Several doors were set into the wall to our right. I led the way to the one marked "Staff Only".

Beyond that door was a corridor that ran in a straight line towards the north wall of the building. On either side were doors, each had a sign above it. We moved down the corridor reading each sign as I looked for the one I wanted. Swimming Pool, Sauna, Locker Room, Staff Room, Store Room and finally Roof Access.

The door was locked which was a good sign. It meant that if we could get through we would be able to reach the roof without other people being in the way. I pulled the claw hammer from my backpack and gestured the others back. The wooden door was most likely locked to stop staff using the roof for smoke breaks, rather than as serious security. A dozen blows against the area I estimated the locking mechanism to be and the door fell open.

A steel ladder bolted to the wall opposite the door was all the room contained. I motioned for the others to follow and started to climb. I kept the hammer to hand which made the climb awkward. It would be needed though if the trapdoor above was locked.

At the top of the ladder I took a moment to check the progress of the others. Claire was directly behind me, followed by Maggie and then Lily brought up the rear gently urging the little girl on. In the dim light I ran my hand around the edge of the trapdoor, feeling for a lock by touch. I found a deadbolt set into the frame beside the ladder and pulled it back before I heaved on the wooden trapdoor.

Light flooded the narrow passage momentarily blinding me, before I climbed through the opening and onto the gym roof. I took a quick glance around to ensure no immediate threats were near before I reached down to help the others through. In moments we were all stood together on the roof.

"So what now?" Lily asked.

"Well now we need a way down." I said looking towards the southern edge of the roof. I couldn't hear any gunfire. Perhaps more alarming, I couldn't hear any screaming which would indicate that no living remained outside the stadium itself. I leaned in close to Claire and quietly said "Best keep Maggie here, she won't want to see what's happening." She nodded and I walked over the roof with Lily in tow.

The large roof area had a black coating of tarpaper and several large aluminium vents rose out of the roof. We reached the edge and immediately dropped to lie flat against the soft and tacky material of the roof. The car park before the south gate was an abattoir.

Beyond the gates, hundreds of corpses lay. In some places they were stacked one atop another where they had been cut down. The gates themselves still stood, the land rovers had provided an effective barricade. The security fence though had failed to stand against the mass, bending inwards in some places while entire panels had fallen in others.

Several soldiers still lay where they had fallen though some were already up and walking around. The tarmac of the car park was littered with the fallen. I could clearly see some zombies feasting on the fresher remains. The majority though seemed to quickly lose interest in dead flesh and headed into the stadium in search of live food.

A countless number of the refugees lay dead, their blood covered the ground and splashed the walls. The largest concentration lay around the entrance. They must have been pushing against each other trying to get in as the zombies came up behind them. Beside me Lily was quietly crying.

I shuffled backwards away from the edge. I awkwardly patted Lily as I inwardly cursed my inability to offer comfort. She looked back at me and wiped her eyes. She seemed to understand that I had tried.

Lily headed back to Claire and her daughter whilst I checked the north and west sides. The north held much of the same, the west though held promise. It seemed the west wall of the gym provided a natural barrier to entry so the security fencing was bolted into the walls to the north and south. Below the roof on the west side was pavement and road. Very few of the undead were in sight. Any that had been here had joined their brethren and were inside now feasting.

I re-joined the others. "We have a way out. The only problem I can see is that we have about twenty feet to drop from the roof to the road." I told them.

"There's no chance we could make that without breaking bones." Lily said with frustration.

"No. Not just dropping. We will need a ladder or a rope, something to help us get closer to the ground at least." I agreed. I glanced towards the trapdoor set into the roof. I really wasn't looking forward to this next bit. "I am going to head back in and see if I can find anything to help us."

"Are you kidding!" said Lily. "You know what it will be like in there."

"We don't have very much choice." I told her, trying to keep my tone firm. "Beside's. I am pretty sick of getting stuck on roofs." I added with a grin.

I handed the hammer and backpack to Lily. "If anyone but me comes up here, feel free to whack them." I said as I lifted the door and cautiously peered within. It seemed clear. I began the long climb down watching the light slowly disappear as the trapdoor above me closed. I dropped the last four feet and fell into a crouch, ready for anyone beyond the doorway. All was clear.

The staff corridor had gained a number of people in the short time I had been above. They pressed together against the door that lead out to the gym. Fear was palpable. The noise of their whispered conversations merged with the screaming and crying from within the gym. Wary of being noticed I crept quietly down the corridor to the door I had previously seen marked as a store room.

The store room door was unlocked and I slipped into the cool dark interior. I fumbled along the wall beside the door for a light switch, finally finding one and flicking it on. The light revealed a room full of shelving. Metal racks lined the walls from floor to ceiling. Two shelving units stood in the centre of the room. Each space on the shelves was filled with spare towels, mats and weights. Boxes of water bottles, plastic wallets for membership cards and spare parts for the various pieces of gym equipment were stacked neatly.

I moved down the shelves peering into boxes and shifting items. Eventually I found what I needed. A box of jump ropes, each one seemed around ten feet including handles. Made of a thin and flexible rubber they weren't ideal but they would perhaps get the job done. I counted five. Fifty feet of lightweight modern material, I hoped it would be enough.

Carrying the box, I pulled open the store room door and peeked through. It seemed things had escalated in the brief time I had been searching the room. The crowd of people were pushing against the doors. Something on the other side was trying extremely hard to get through. It was definitely time to leave.

Giving up any pretence of stealth I ran for the ladder. I managed to climb one handed the box tucked under my arm and I banged my elbow against the trapdoor when I reached the top. It opened slowly to reveal Lily stood above, hammer raised. She let out a yelp of relief as she saw me, throwing back the trapdoor and reaching to help me through.

I explained the plan with the others. We took the jump ropes and tied two knots in each, trying to keep the distance between even. That task done I began to tie each of them, one to another. We lost some length from the knots and the necessity of making them secure. We could still have perhaps forty feet or so of a makeshift rope.

We carried it to the edge and I let one end fall over to hit the floor below with a thud. As I stood holding the end of our rope and only hope of escape, I realised we had a problem.

We had nothing to secure it to on the roof. I began to swear loudly.

Chapter 10

It would have been pleasant to be able to sit and moan about how bad things were, but to be honest, I was tired of sitting on rooftops. I was tired of reacting to the undead. It was time to be proactive. It was time to act.

I stood on the edge of the roof and looked around. The road that ran beneath me travelled generally from north to south. Across the road sat a public house, two stories of stone. A small beer garden was enclosed in a wooden fence. Beside the pub was a row of terraced houses each house quiet with no movement behind their windows.

The houses continued to the north until the road turned a corner. The road had a great many vehicles parked along its length. In places some of the vehicles that had likely been abandoned had been pushed aside by the military to allow their patrols to drive through. I studied each vehicle as I tried to find one that was suitable. Eventually I found what I was searching for. It sat pushed onto the curb and against a wall. The passenger side door was open.

"Lily." I called.

"What's up?" she asked as she walked across the roof to join me. I pointed to the vehicle I had chosen. "Do you think you can start that if I can get you off the roof?" I asked her.

"Sure." She said after a moment. "But why?"

I quickly outlined my idea. Lily smiled and agreed. I called Claire and her daughter over.

"Ok. Claire, you and I are going to hold onto this end of the jump ropes." I said, holding up the end of the rope as I did so. "We are going to hold tight so Lily can climb down. She will then head over to that van." I pointed at the large grey transit van I had seen.

"What good will that do?" Claire asked.

"That van is perhaps seven or eight feet high. Lily can drive it alongside the wall directly beneath us. I can hold the rope and lower you and Maggie down, but with no way to secure it I would be stuck. With the van beneath me I think I can hang from this roof ledge and I won't have so far to drop." I told her with a smile.

"Ok." She said as she grabbed hold of our makeshift rope. I was fine with her taking the end. I would stand at the edge and take the majority of the weight on the rope. I got into position and braced myself, right foot pressed up against the small raised lintel that ran along the edge of the roof.

Lily wrapped the line around her waist and sat on the edge of the roof. She took a deep breath and gave me a nervous smile before taking a firm hold on our rope and lowering herself over the edge.

She was in no way large for her size but trying to support the full weight of an adult was harder than I had imagined. The thin rubber rope dug painfully into my flesh as I leaned back to avoid being pulled over. It must have taken less than a minute but that minute stretched painfully for me as I tried to hold myself in an unaccustomed position, muscles aching from the strain.

Finally the line went slack. I looked over the edge in time to see Lily wave before she sprinted towards the van. I waited impatiently and watched her reach the back of the vehicle. She was cautious, taking her time to look around before approaching the door. I saw her poke her head through the open door and held my breath. If anything was in there, now would be the time to grab her. She looked back towards us and gave a wave that I hoped meant all clear before she climbed into the cab of the van.

Shouting from the open hatch caught my attention. I jogged across the roof to see what was happening. I reached the trapdoor just as a man climbed out. I skidded to a stop with a curse.

"Help us, quick" he yelled at me as he reached down into the passageway.

I peered down through the opening. The ladder held two women and a man. I couldn't see below them but I could hear enough to know that zombies were crowding the bottom of the ladder. This was a complication I didn't need. I looked across at Claire. She was busy looking towards the van. I considered throwing this man back down at his friends and closing the trapdoor. Maggie turned her head and saw us. She pulled on her mother's arm and pointed. Damn. I couldn't do it with them watching.

I reached into the gap and helped the newcomer pull up his friends, one after another. When the final man had climbed out we slammed shut the trapdoor. I didn't think the zombies could climb but it wasn't worth risking.

"Thanks for the help" Said the first man. He held his hand out towards me, "Names Mike. Thought we were done for there."

I reluctantly shook his hand. "These are Rachel, Ellie and Patrick." Mike said pointing at each in turn. I nodded once to them as their names were called.

"Ryan." I said, "Maggie and Claire" I pointed.

"Really pleased to meet you all. I hope you have a way down, it's all gone to hell down there." Mike said.

"Working on it." I responded reluctantly before trotting back to Claire and Maggie.

"How's Lily doing?" I asked Claire.

"Van's not moving yet." She replied sounding scared. I gave her a pat on the shoulder. I hoped I was getting better at providing comfort but doubted it. I looked towards the van. It was still and quiet. I hoped that meant Lily was making progress in the cab.

"Blimey that's a bit of a drop" Mike said as he reached us and looked down. "We all climbing down that rope?"

"No."

"Then what's the plan?" He asked, his brow furrowed in puzzlement.

"Our friend Lily is going to bring a van so we can drop down" Claire said. She was looking at Mike from the corner of her eye, she had an appraising look. Great, that would be yet another complication we wouldn't need.

Claire and the new folk exchanged names as we waited. She took the time to ask what had happened and made various sounds as they told their tale. I was feeling sulky. I didn't like large groups and was just getting used to the people in this one. Too many people around me at once was incredibly stressful and a nuisance I didn't need. If nothing else it would make me irritable in a way that only a kill could help.

The faint sound of an engine coming to life brought my attention back to the van. I saw an arm reach out and pull the door shut before it slowly reversed away from the pavement. Lily had come through for us. In minutes she had the van turned around and was parked beneath us.

"Right then. I'll hold the rope whilst you climb down" I said to Claire.

"Why bother with the rope?" interrupted Mike. "If Pat and I hang down, the drop to the roof isn't far and we can catch the rest of you."

"That's a great idea." Claire positively gushed. Mike set about directing his friends. In a short time he and Patrick had dropped to the roof. Maggie was gently lowered down to their waiting arms. Claire followed and then Rachel and Ellie. I went over the edge last. I hung from the ledge and pushed off to the side to land at the back of the van, disdaining their offers of help.

I climbed off the van and approached Lily who was in the process of being introduced to the newcomers. "Good work." I said as I gave Lily a smile.

"Thanks. What now?" She asked.

"We stick to the original plan, we head north to the Lakes but we will need supplies first."

"What's in the Lakes?" Mike interrupted again. "Why not find somewhere in town to hole up?"

"Look around you. That idea hasn't worked so well so far has it?" I told him.

"Tell you what. I worked on a farm a few years ago. We should head there." Mike said, looking around for support.

"You can head wherever you like. We have somewhere else to go."

"No, no. Let's go to the farm. We can at least have a breather there before doing anything else." Patrick chimed in as Rachel and Ellie offered their support.

"We could do that" Claire said looking to Lily. "It makes sense. We won't get far without some food and stuff anyway." She added.

"Right then. It's decided. You lot jump in the back and I'll drive us." Mike spoke with determination. His friends were already on the move to the back of the van. Patrick climbed in the passenger side of the cab. Lily looked at me helplessly and shrugged.

"Guess we are going to this farm then." She said as she followed the others. Claire and Maggie were already moving. In moments it was just me, stood on the road. Mike leaned out of the van window and asked, "you coming?"

It seemed I had little choice. I climbed into the back of the van pulling closed the door behind me. The van had just a few bits of loose carpeting covered in dust and muck and some empty boxes. They had been shifted around to allow the group to sit on the floor. It wouldn't be comfortable but it was dry and zombie free.

I sat beside Lily as the van set off. The group chatted about their lives and what they were doing when this whole thing had started. It had not taken them long to grow used to the horrors of this new world. Just a short while ago they had been running from their lives and faced death and rebirth as a zombie. Now while safe they could laugh again.

Stuck in the back of the van with nothing to do, I took the time to look over each of my new companions in turn. Rachel had red shoulder length hair in a pony tail. She was young, perhaps early twenties. She was wearing Jeans and a vest top that once may have been white. A small bag with a thin strap was thrown over her shoulder.

Ellie looked to be around the same age as Rachel. I had the feeling they had known each other before all this. She sat close to her friend and laughed easily. She wore dusty black leggings and a baggy shirt of some kind. Hair dark, almost black hung loose around her face. She sported several piercings and a tattoo of some kind adorned the back of her neck.

I had never understood the urge to pierce or tattoo your body. I had never encountered anything that I wanted to have inked into my skin for the rest of my life. Piercings just seemed pointless, like most jewellery. It served no purpose except to draw people's attention to you. I had spent the better part of my life actively working to be as unnoticeable as possible.

Patrick it seemed was eager to follow Mikes lead. He wasn't very tall, perhaps five and a half feet but he was solidly built. I imagined he had been hiding in the gym as that place was where he had spent all his time anyway. He had the look of someone who worked out a lot, but the muscles were all for show. As was the fake tan that was already fading and the shaven head that was slowly sprouting new hair.

Mike was all confidence. He was used to being the leader and he irritated me. He had stepped in and taken over my little group with little fuss. I wasn't used to being in charge, so had no real way of dealing with threats to my leadership. He was a very handsome man and had certainly caught the attention of Claire. He was naturally tanned and in good physical shape. Dark hair cut short and in what I imagined to be a fashionable cut. He sat in the driver's seat laughing at some comment from Patrick. I had a brief imagining of what it would feel like to run a knife blade across his throat and felt my heart beat a little faster.

But that wasn't to be. I had made a promise and as annoying as he may be, I would hold to my word. I couldn't kill him. I would however have to find some way to take control of this group again. I liked Lily and was used to having her around, not to mention the fact that she had proved herself both capable and effective. I would stick with her, but I wasn't going to be a happy little follower of Mike.

We drove for about an hour. Through the windshield I watched the suburban area turn to countryside. It seemed as though the majority of zombies had been busy feasting within the stadium. We saw few on the roads. Those zombies that we did see Mike would aim for, clipping them with the corner of the van and laughing as they were thrown across the road. Eventually he pulled up beside a thick wooden gate and shut off the engine.

"Right folks. We are going to be walking from here. This van won't get down the path to the farm. It's not built for it." He called.

"Are the farmer and his family going to be here?" Lily asked.

"Most likely but don't worry, I know him and I am sure they won't turn us away." Mike said as he climbed out of the cab.

The rest of the group followed. Patrick of course following close behind like a puppy. Rachel and Ellie linked arms and walked along as though it were any normal day, whilst Claire and Maggie walked beside Lily talking quietly. I brought up the rear alone and excluded.

Many people when asked will tell you that they love to get out of the town and into the countryside whenever possible. If you ask them why, they will explain in great detail that it is full of life, the air is cleaner and much nonsense like that. I had been in the countryside for ten minutes and I was already thinking fondly of the zombie filled town.

The farm was situated atop a hill so the wind had nothing to block it and it was cold. I could not say whether the air was cleaner but it certainly smelt a great deal more like manure than the air I was used to. The nice and firm paved streets had been replaced by a long path of wet mud and of course what looked to be horse manure. I was not in a good mood by the time we reached the farm itself.

This farm consisted of a two story stone house with a small lawn and a peaked stone tile roof covered in moss. The building was old and had probably been in the care of one family for generations. A large rickety looking barn made of wood and a stone stable that currently stood empty completed the farm yard. The whole place was quiet. Mike jogged up to the door and knocked. No one answered. Patrick had climbed through the small flower bed and was peering through a window into the darkened interior.

"Can't see anyone pal." Patrick called to Mike who acknowledged with a wave and reached for the door handle. The door opened with no resistance and Mike walked into the house.

"That probably isn't a good idea." Lily said as she turned to me. I just shrugged. If he wanted to get himself killed then that would solve one of my problems.

"You should go with him" she added.

"Why? He seems happy enough to do it himself." I hated how sulky I sounded. Lily picked up on it too. "What's wrong with you?"

"Oh you know, zombie apocalypse. People we don't know who are suddenly deciding where we go and what we are doing. The usual." I said with forced cheer. It didn't seem to fool her.

"Fine then, you stand out here and I will go help." Lily said with a shake of her head before she walked across the yard to the front door. I watched her enter, pausing to call out first before disappearing inside. I fidgeted and rubbed my arms. A t-shirt wasn't the best attire for standing out in the cold wind.

I was concerned for Lily. I didn't doubt her ability to look after herself but I had no idea how Mike would react if they encountered the undead as they searched. Lily still had my hammer at least. A cry came from within the house. I cursed and ran across the muddy yard.

The door opened into a large modern kitchen. Sturdy cupboards and a large oven filled one wall. An old rectangular wooden table filled the centre of the floor with six chairs placed around it. Two doors stood open and led out of the room, beyond the first doorway were a set of steps that led upwards. I could hear noise from above and shot up the stairs.

The sound was louder from the landing at the top of the stairs. Several doors lined the hall and I headed for the one that stood open. The cause of the noise was immediately apparent. An old man dressed in plain blue pyjamas was on top of Lily struggling to reach her with his teeth. Lily had both hands on the hammer that was pressed under his chin. I saw the strain on her arms as she pushed with all her strength as she tried to keep the walking corpse away.

I cast my gaze around the room. It was the main bedroom, a double bed filled the centre of the room. Wardrobes and chests of drawers lined the walls at either side. A window filled the wall above the bed. I could see nothing that I could use as a weapon. With little choice I stepped behind the zombie and reached down to wrap my arms around his throat and pulled him backwards.

With the pressure on her arms lifted, Lily scrambled out from beneath the zombie. "Hit it anytime you want" I called to her as I struggled to maintain my grip. She raised her hammer a look of determination crossing her face. I closed my eyes and turned my head away whilst trying to hold the zombie steady. The last thing I wanted was to have infected blood splash into my eyes or mouth.

The zombie jerked in my arms as Lily's first blow hit true. A second followed and then a third. With each blow of her hammer I felt more fluid land on my flesh.

"It's dead. It's not moving" Lily said to me. I released my hold and let it fall lifeless once more to the floor. I felt behind me for the bed, eyes and mouth still closed and sat down.

"You look a mess, stay there. Don't move" She instructed. I heard her leave the room as the pounding of feet running up the stairs echoed through the house. A conversation followed too low for me to hear. I was sitting in an unfamiliar house with my eyes closed, unable to speak and with a dead body at my feet. It was not a pleasant feeling.

All of a sudden, those little sounds that you would hear every day were magnified. My imagination ran wild. That creak of a floorboard became the zombie wife of the farmer as she came looking for her husband. The sound a door made as it opened, was close. Perhaps in the room, was it a zombie coming from the closet. I admit that I jumped as I felt someone touch my hand.

"It's ok Ryan. It's me." Lily's voice was immeasurably soothing as she took my hand in hers, skin warm and comforting. "Don't try and speak and don't open your eyes. You are covered in blood. The others are boiling some water. We need to get you clean."

I nodded, that was all I could do. I had begun to worry that I could feel the infection seeping into my skin. I was in no way a germaphobe but I had always had a healthy understanding of the bacteria and infections I could pick up through contact with others, especially considering my choice of pastime. The feeling I had as I felt the fluids slowly run down my face was something close to terror. I held tight to Lily's hand.

Several eternities passed as I sat there and waited. Lily spoke soothingly to me in a low and calm tone. She spoke of her life before all of this, of family and friends. She told me how she had been working in a bar and considering college and a career, though she didn't know what she had wanted to do.

Her voice lowered and she spoke quietly of the shock she had felt when she realised that I was a killer. She admitted that she was going to leave me and not look back when we arrived at somewhere safe enough for her to do so. She stopped talking for a moment and I wanted desperately to speak, to ask why then she had left the stadium with me.

I heard her sigh and felt her body shake where she was pressed against me beside the bed. I realised she was crying. She stood abruptly as someone came up the stairs and released my hand. A moment later I heard one of the girls speak as she entered the room. Rachel or Ellie, I wasn't familiar enough to recognise them by voice alone.

"Ok. We have some boiled water here. They said they put some disinfectant in so hopefully we can get you clean safely" Lily told me as she placed something heavy beside me on the bed.

"It will be hot, sorry." She said as she gently wiped around my eyes. The water was painfully hot. In a short time though, she was done. "There. I think you can open your eyes now." Lily said.

My eyes opened slowly and I had to blink several times as the light filled them. Lily sat in front of me smiling, the rag she had been using to clean me held in her hand. Her eyes were red.

"Thank you." I said, my mouth was dry and a little croaky. Lily smiled and stood.

"The other guys have cleared the house. Mike said he hasn't found the wife, but their truck is missing so she was probably in town."

I nodded slowly. "Where are they now?"

"Downstairs. Claire is making some food and the others are trying to get the TV to work." Lily replied.

"Thank you for letting me come with you. At the stadium I mean. You didn't have to." I told her. I thought it was important to say that.

"I was happy to see you" she said after a small pause. "I was upset when I thought you had been killed because I asked you to help Claire and Maggie."

"That was my choice."

"Perhaps, but if you were on your own you wouldn't have risked it would you?"

"No. Probably not" I admitted.

She sat beside me on the bed once more. "When you didn't turn up and I thought you were dead, Brian had shown how useless he was. Despite your being... what you are, you at least had risked your own life to save mine and others.

When we got to the stadium all I could find were people who were out for themselves. Everyone was so desperate to ensure their own safety with no care for others." She paused and gave me another of her radiant smiles.

"I realised that we all have our faults. Yours might be fairly major." She laughed and after a moment's thought, I did too. "You are who and what you are Ryan, but you at least have been willing to help me and others. We wouldn't have even got out of that stadium if it wasn't for you."

"So you are not thinking of heading off on your own then?"

"No. Everything has gone to hell. We need all the help we can get. Stick to our agreement and we will be fine." Lily said with a smile. "Now come on. Let's go see if we can get something to eat and have a look around, you really do need some clean clothes."

I had to agree. My clothes were speckled with a variety of fresh fluids. I pushed myself to my feet. "What about him?" I asked pointing at the corpse on the floor.

"Mike and Pat can get rid of it. They may as well do something useful." Lily said as she walked from the room. It seemed she at least hadn't fallen for Mikes charms. I followed her from the room as a small smile tugged at my lips.

Chapter 11

Downstairs we found Claire working happily over the stove. Maggie was sat quietly at the kitchen table. Lily poked her head through the door into the living room to ask Mike and Pat to shift the dead farmer before sitting beside Maggie at the table.

A glance through the door told me that the other girls were sat watching the news. It was pretty much the same thing I had been watching days ago in the flat. I figured it was on a loop and would just keep going till the power went out.

"Has anyone checked the barn and stables" I asked Claire, who just shook her head in the negative and continuing with her cooking.

"Guess I will then since I am already caked in muck" I offered.

"You do that and I'll see if anything in the wardrobes will fit you" Lily said.

I stepped into the yard. A fine mist of cold rain speckled my exposed skin in the low evening light. We were well into October and before long this rain would turn to sleet and then snow and ice. After the mild summer the experts had all been predicting a rough winter. Any day now we would likely lose power and gas. Most likely water pressure too. It would get bad.

As I walked across the muddy yard to the barn I was considering what we would need. Clothes obviously and food, bottled water and some way to purify any water we came across of course. Perhaps bottled gas and heaters, a generator would be nice. The list was growing too big. The more people we needed to look after the harder it would be. It was all the more reason then, to cut our numbers down a little. The problem of course would be doing it without breaking the promise I had made to Lily.

The barn was big and old. The cracked and warped wood of the walls, offered little barrier to the elements. Dark stains covered the wood and a small pool of rainwater had formed at the base of one wall. A number of rusted farm implements were attached to hooks along the wall. Old bottles, tyres and other odds and ends had found their way into the barn to be forgotten. Dust covered cobwebs covered nearly everything.

One piece of luck, a small hatchet lay amongst the old junk. I wiped off the dust and picked it up. It was a little rusted and definitely blunt. The handle was old but still firm. I swung it a few times to feel the weight. It would do nicely as a weapon. I could find nothing else of value so I left to go and check the stables that were attached to the back of the farmhouse.

The first thing I noticed about the stables was the smell. Old straw covered the floor of the two stalls that were all the low stone building held. A plastic bucket still sat in one of the stalls, full of water long since turned stagnant. I had no idea what had happened to the horses but they hadn't been here for a little while. I could see nothing of use to us so left the stables and headed back into the house. I paused before the door to wipe most of the mud off of my shoes.

Lily met me as I stepped through the door. She was wearing a dark green bathrobe and had a thick blue robe in her arms. "Hey. I don't think any of his clothes will fit you. Put this on and give me your clothes. I'll put them in the washing machine for you. May as well use it while we have electric." She said as she handed me the robe.

"Better be quick, Claire is about to serve some pasta" she added.

At the thought of food my stomach gave an embarrassingly loud rumble, which caused Maggie to look up and burst into giggles. It was nice to see her smile. I went up the stairs in search of a bathroom.

By the time I had found one, stripped and washed up, Claire was calling everyone to the table. I headed down the stairs and paused at the bottom, bemused by a scene of friendly chaos as six adults and a child all tried to serve themselves at the same time. Lily stepped up and shortly had everyone standing in line as she filled bowls with long strands of pasta and a thick red sauce.

Mike and his friends carried their bowls into the living room where they had seemingly staked a claim. Claire sat with Maggie at the table with a smile as she watched the little girl wolf down the food. Lily with a smile placed a bowl on the table and told me to sit as she took my soiled clothing and put them in the washing machine with her own equally soiled clothes.

She set the washing machine to work and satisfied that her domestic chores were done, joined us at the table with a bowl of pasta for herself. The food was simple but tasty with enough left for the little girl to have seconds.

As we ate we discussed our options. Mike and Pat had claimed the living room to sleep in, with the central heating on and some blankets they had found in an airing cupboard on the second floor they would be cosy enough. The farmhouse had three bedrooms. Two had belonged to the farmer's children, they were small rooms but Rachel and Ellie were happy to stay in one.

Claire and Maggie would take the second room as neither wanted to sleep in the master bedroom the farmer had been found in. Lily believed that the farmer must have been one of those who had the original flu like bug and had died in his sleep. Whilst the mattress was not totally ruined, it would certainly need a good clean and would be better turned. The blankets and sheets that were on the bed would be burned.

The whole room would need a scrub down before it was habitable, so she would sleep on the floor in Claire and Maggie's room. The living room floor with Mike and Pat had very little appeal but the only other option would be the kitchen floor which was tiled and no doubt uncomfortably cold. I decided to sleep on the living room floor.

Decisions made, Claire and Maggie went to their room. It had been a long and exhausting day. I stayed to help Lily wash and dry the dishes as we waited for our clothes to finish in the machine.

"We will need to have a proper inventory of food tomorrow" Lily said as we sat back down at the table.

"Not just the food. We will need to find containers to fill with water."

"How long do you think before we will need them?" she asked.

"To be honest I am surprised we still have water and power. I think we are on borrowed time with them."

A frown appeared on Lily's brow, lips pursed as she considered. "So what do we do when the water stops?"

"Well. We will need to find another source and purify it. For a little while at least we will possibly be able to find some bottled water in houses and any shops that we can reach."

"You want us to steal bottled water?" Lily asked with surprise.

"I don't think its stealing so much as making use of things that will just be wasted otherwise." I said. "It's not like we will have to worry about the police."

"I suppose not. How do we purify water anyway? Will boiling it be enough?"

"I have no idea." I laughed. "We will need to find a library or a working computer with internet and a printer."

Lily groaned. "Another library. Really! I would have thought once was enough."

"Perhaps a smaller one this time, and we will be better prepared" I told her. "Besides we will need to know more than just how to purify water. Food is going to be a priority soon."

Mike entered the kitchen followed by Pat and sat at the table uninvited. "TV station just went offline. Just getting snow now" he said.

"It was bound to happen sooner or later." I replied. "You said you worked here before. How well do you know the area?"

"Well enough. Why?"

"Supplies. We will need some which means someone has to go and take a look at any shops that we can get to." I told him. A thought occurred and I added, "Perhaps you, me and Pat can go get a look and see what we can find tomorrow."

Mike nodded slowly. "Sure. There's a petrol station a couple of miles from here in the village. I think they had a corner shop too."

"One of those big supermarkets was built last year as well" Patrick added.

We spent the next fifteen minutes discussing what we would need to get. Rachel and Ellie came into the kitchen to let us know they were off to try and sleep and Lily soon followed. I sat back in the chair for a while as Mike and Pat talked. I had some plans of my own to make. I said goodnight and went to find a place to curl up in the living room.

I awoke before dawn the next day. A restless night on the hard floor had left me with a sharp pain in my neck whenever I turned my head. I roused myself and paid a visit to the bathroom. I was dismayed to find no toothbrush and mentally added that to the list of needed supplies. My mouth had gone several days now without seeing a brush and I had the distinct feeling that my breath would smell as rancid as it tasted.

No one else was yet awake so I retrieved the hatchet I had found yesterday and slipped on my shoes then went out into the yard to look for something to sharpen it. The sun was just beginning to rise, the darkness retreating. The world around the farm was still and quiet, dew heavy grasses waved in a light breeze. It was almost enough to make you forget about the apocalypse that had engulfed the world.

A squelching sound followed me as I crossed the yard. The rain that had arrived late yesterday had reduced the already muddy yard to a quagmire. The only bonus I could see was that I would hear any undead wandering around long before I saw them.

I had a fruitless search for a sharpening tool in the barn and was left with little choice but to laboriously run the blade back and forth against the rough stone of the stable wall. It made a mess of the wall and took a considerable amount of time but I did finally get a bit more of an edge to the head of the hatchet. I would not be splitting hairs with it, but it would make a mess of any zombies I encountered.

Whilst I worked I had spent my time trying to think of ways to reduce our parties number on this little trip into the village. I had yet to come up with anything definite and it looked like I would be forced to come up with something on the fly. That was certainly not my preferred way of working. I went back to the house to get dressed.

The house was still and quiet by the time I was ready to go. My attempts to rouse Mike and Pat were ineffectual. Bored and annoyed I rooted noisily through the kitchen. Nothing jumped out at me as really useful, though I did find a writing pad and some paper so spent the next thirty minutes writing down lists of all the items I thought we would need.

By the time the first member of our little group was awake, I had finished my lists and was busily making a large pot of porridge whilst a dozen rashers of bacon were slowly cooking in the oven and filling the kitchen with a most delightful odour.

Maggie was the first to join me, she bounded down the stairs full of energy and good cheer in a way the few adults could manage first thing on a morning. Claire and Lily soon followed smiling appreciatively at my cooking efforts.

"Where did you find bacon?" Claire asked with a wide smile.

"There were a couple of packs in the bottom of the freezer" I said and pointed at the small chest freezer in the corner of the room. "We will need to start using the food in there first, save the cans and packaged stuff for when the power goes."

The girls nodded and joined Maggie at the table. I filled a bowl with porridge and dropped a few rashers of bacon hot from the oven onto a plate before placing it on the table before the little girl.

"Here you go little lady. You get to have the first taste of my cooking." I said with a wink and my largest possible grin. The shy little girl smiled and tucked in to the food. It was nice to see her smile. I had always appreciated the younger children. Teens irritated me and adults were of little worth, but the younger children, well they had an innocence and general joy with life that I rarely encountered and I appreciated it when I did.

After filling bowls for the others we sat and talked about our plans for the day. Maggie finished her food and I passed her the notepad and pen to keep her entertained. I read through the list I had prepared and Lily quickly added a few more items that the girls would appreciate. I looked at the list and thought that the first thing we would need to loot would be a dozen bags.

Lily and Claire were going to strip and scrub clean the master bedroom. If the weather stayed clear they would wash as much clothing as they could and have it hung out to dry. I reminded them that we would need an inventory of food and received glares from the girls and a scathing reminder that they were not stupid and knew what was needed.

I felt it would be a good time to forcibly get the guys up and moving so retreated from the table. Mike and Pat were reluctant to move, but with enough prodding and some cursing they were fed and ready to leave. We said our goodbyes to the rest of the group and I retrieved my hatchet as we set out across the yard and along the muddy track to where we had parked the van.

Mike climbed into the driver's seat after a quick check to ensure we were zombie free. Pat took the passenger side and I was left to climb once more into the back. As I tried to find a comfortable place to sit Mike said, "We are running low on diesel. Should have enough to get us to the village but if we don't find any there we will be walking back."

"Well let's make the petrol station our first stop then." I suggested.

A grunt was my only reply as the van roared to life and we were on our way.

Sat in the back of the van I was largely ignored on the short trip to the village. Mike and Pat chatted and laughed at this and that, whilst I sat with hatchet in hand and wondered which of them we would be returning without.

We arrived at a small petrol station set on the edge of the village. I climbed from the van and stretched. Even a short trip had been unpleasant. Around us spread fields of short grass surrounded by low walls of dark stone. A dozen shaggy white sheep lay in one field. Their bodies still, splashes of crimson covered their forms. It was the first proof I had seen that the undead would attack prey other than humans.

The petrol station itself was a simple one story building with large glass windows that looked onto a dark interior. Two fuel pumps sat on the forecourt, the signs indicated one was petrol, the other diesel. A couple of zombies had noticed our arrival and were slowly shuffling towards us.

I was struck again by the differences in the undead I had encountered. Some were fast, vicious and almost intelligent, a very real threat. Others like these before me, through injury or some consequence of whatever had resurrected them were slow and stupid. I had an urge to test my hatchet so quietly moved ahead of the guys, arms to the side and weapon at the ready.

The undead were both walking stiffly, arms outstretched and mouth opened wide to reveal their broken teeth. Blood covered them liberally and they each bore a number of deep wounds across their necks and faces. I Paused and took a slow deep breath and tightened my grip.

As the lead zombie reached half dozen paces from where I stood I leapt at him. A sweep of my arm knocked aside his arms as I struck his temple with my hatchet. Bone crunched and a small amount of fluid splashed, as it fell without a sound.

The second was upon me, its hands formed into claws dug painfully into my left arm. I lashed out with my weapon cutting deeply into the side of its neck. A second blow jarred against the spine. A third heavy strike and the spine severed, the zombies head fell to one side and it lost whatever rudimentary control it had over its body.

The whole fight had taken less than a minute and I stood breathing heavily, eyes darting back and forth looking for any other threat. Finding none I turned my attention to the hands clasped painfully to my arm. I prised the fingers apart and inspected my arm. The skin was thankfully unbroken. I would need to get a jacket soon, it was not a good idea to be fighting the undead in a t-shirt.

"That was incredible" said Pat as he walked over to stand beside me. "I really need to get some kind of weapon too". I flashed him a grin. I had enjoyed it a great deal.

Mike just gave a grunt frowning as he got back into the van. I was rapidly coming to the belief that our friend Mike was a bit of a coward. He had been nowhere to be found when Lily was being attacked in the house and had happily hung back here. It was also painfully clear from the way he was looking at me that he didn't like my showing him up. I smiled. I could use his ego and cowardice against him.

The pumps were still working and had plenty of fuel available. Once more the fact that we still had power in this area was to our benefit. I left Mike to drive up to the pumps and fill the van and gestured Pat to follow me to check out the building.

The glass doors opened manually and currently stood closed. I banged on the glass a couple of times to see if anything stirred within but all seemed quiet. I pushed open the door and led the way in.

Inside the building was in disarray. Someone had been through already. The till stood open with the money missing. Someone stupid had been through already then. We checked the aisles. It didn't take long and the only things we could find were various chocolate bars and sugary junk. I looked behind the counter and found a small box filled with plastic bags. I opened one out and threw in some sweets and chocolate bars for Maggie. The cigarette racks and booze shelves were all empty.

Mike called to us from the van, we climbed back in. Pat took his seat in the passenger side whilst I sat in the back once more.

"We are full and ready to go." Mike said.

"Village shop first and then supermarket?" I asked the guys.

"Sure. Best to take it slow though, no idea what it will be like in the village proper" Pat said.

I nodded thoughtfully. Even a small village would likely have a couple of thousand people. Someone had also looted the petrol station and could still be around. I sat back against the side of the van barely registering the vibration as the engine came to life. We would need to be wary.

Chapter 12

The village was a curious mixture of old stone buildings and their newer brick counterparts. Nestled between two large hills, the houses were neat with well tended gardens and streets. It was large enough to warrant two public houses and a supermarket. Few places of business were close by, so the majority of people who lived here would have had to commute to work.

We reached the village centre with no bother. Few zombies were around, those that were in the road had made a few new dents in the front bumper but caused no problems. Mike pulled up outside the village shop that stood opposite a pub with a sign above the door that proudly proclaimed it to be the 'Black Bull' public house. I felt a small surge of excitement as I saw the vehicle parked in front of us.

We clambered out of the van and stood in a loose clump in front of the van. Mike wanted to check out the pub but after a brief argument agreed that we would do that last. I pointed to the vehicle and told them we needed to check that out too.

"Why do you want to look at a mobile book van?" Pat asked.

"It'll have some books I want to look at, besides we can pick a few up for Maggie to keep the poor kid entertained." I told them. Mike looked disinterested and just shrugged his shoulders. Pat agreed to help me after we had been through the shop.

Hatchet in hand I led the way to the shop. I paused once again at the doorway and tapped loudly on the door. Silence from within. I stepped through the door and immediately saw why. The shops small selection of fresh vegetables, were spread across the floor slowly soaking in the large pool of blood that came from the lady who lay quite dead before the counter.

It seemed a great deal of blood for a zombie. I crouched beside the body. The lady who must have been in her late fifties when alive, lay face down on the floor. She had a number of small cuts and bruising about her face. At least two of her fingers were broken and the side of her skull had been caved in by some kind of blunt instrument. She had fought her attackers but I was certain she had not been undead when her skull was crushed.

"No booze or cigarettes. Money is gone too" said Pat from behind the counter. The looters were murderers as well it would seem. We searched the shop for anything we could use. Mike found some canvas bags and we managed to fill them with some canned goods that had been ignored. In the back storeroom I found a couple of large twelve kilo bags of potatoes and some candles. I carried it all out to the van.

We were wary now. The lady in the shop had been dead a short while, likely killed in the last couple of days. The looters were possibly holed up in this village or somewhere close. After a brief consultation Mike went into the pub whilst Pat came to help me with my search of the book mobile as promised.

The book mobiles had been around for years. Run by the local council they ensured outlying villages could have access to a library without actually needing to build one. They were also used to bring the libraries to areas with a high elderly population. The selection would be smaller but I hoped we would find something of use.

A mobile library was the length of a single decker bus. It had no need of windows along the side as the interior was filled floor to ceiling with shelving. A section at the front would contain the driver's area and a counter and terminal for people to visit and check out any books that they fancied. A door sat approximately half way down the side of the vehicle. Pat and I made for that.

The door was open with bloody swipe marks around the edges. We approached cautiously as Pat gestured that I should be the first to enter since I had the weapon. I couldn't really fault the logic and would not relinquish the hatchet so I readied myself to enter.

Once again I found myself knocking on the door frame. No sound came from within. I entered swiftly, head swinging painfully from side to side as I tried to check everywhere at once. All was quiet and I released a breath I hadn't even been aware I was holding.

I called Pat forward and he came inside carrying a few bags from the shop. I directed him to the children's section at the back of the vehicle and he started pulling books from the shelves for Maggie. I moved quickly through the shelves of the non-fiction side. I pulled any book that I thought would be of use and stuffed it into a bag. In a short time I had two bags packed full of books. I grunted as I lifted them and carried them across to the van were Pat was already moving items around, stacking things neatly.

"You mind going to grab Mike?" Pat asked as he took the bags from me.

"Sure, back in a minute" I said and headed to the pub.

The front door was locked so I followed the path around to the back. As I walked I could hear a voice calling for help. I approached the back of the building carefully, alert for danger. I peered around the corner and saw Mike struggling to hold a door closed, moaning and damaged limbs came from behind the door. Straining against the door Mikes eyes widened as he saw me.

"Help! Quick!" he shouted.

"How many are there?" I asked approaching slowly.

"Four or five, does it fucking matter. Help me!" Mike yelled, voice rising in panic.

I readied my weapon and stepped up behind Mike. I struck the back of his knee with the blunt side of the hatchet and jumped back as Mike screamed and collapsed to the ground. The door opened and a pack of zombies spilled out scrambling over one another to leap on Mike. His scream of shock and pain turned to agony as the first teeth found his flesh.

As three of the zombies feasted, two turned their attention to me. I struck one above the eye, shattering bone and splattering brains and blood across the floor before me. It fell without a sound. The second was faster. It leapt towards me in bounds. I took a swipe and caught it high on the shoulder. It was thrown off balance but recovered quickly.

I swung again and knocked another lunge aside with a blow to the zombies right elbow. The damage was ignored and it just kept on coming. I was starting to think that I had made a mistake when Pat came barrelling around the corner with a brick in each hand. The zombie went down with a final moan as Pat beat it about the head with the bricks.

Mike's screams had stopped as his throat was torn out and he lay still. The three that had been feasting on his flesh turned their attention to us. Pat screamed in rage as he saw his friend and ran at the undead as he used his strength to good effect. As he distracted them I was free to assault them from the side, I rained blows upon their skulls. Soon all was still.

Pat sat amongst the carnage, beside his friend as tears ran down his cheeks. I leant against the wall as small shudders ran through my body. I wanted to laugh and shout. I had to fight to keep the grin from forming as I tried to look solemn and upset for Mike's death. I reached out and placed a hand on Pat's shoulder.

"You should go wait by the van." I said.

He brushed a hand across his eyes before looking at me. "Why? We need to bury Mike."

"Mike was killed by zombies. He is going to come back as one of them. You don't need to see that." I said. "You go wait by the van and I will deal with it so you don't have to."

Pat sniffed and looked down at his friend. He slowly climbed to his feet and mumbled a thank you before leaving me alone with just the dead.

I let the smile come now. I had stuck to my word. I had not killed Mike myself. I glanced around at the zombies and quietly chastised myself. I had been too eager, too sure that I would be able to handle the situation and almost gotten myself killed. I was incredibly tempted to let Mike rise before killing him again but wasn't sure how long it would take. Instead I settled for leaving him. It would amuse me to know that he was wandering around as a zombie, that stupid arrogant grin wiped off his face.

As I approached the front of the pub and the van I struggled to assume a more sombre expression. I was brought up short as I rounded the corner. Pat knelt on the road, an unfamiliar youth in jeans and a hoody stood beside him with a knife pressed against his throat. A second teen who seemed barely old enough to shave had been hidden pressed against the wall a baseball bat at the ready which he swung at my midriff. I fell to the floor hatchet dropped from my hand as I doubled over in pain gasping for breath.

I felt myself lifted roughly to my knees to face the youth with the knife. He seemed to be the leader. A third man jumped down from the back of the van and spoke to the leader. "Not much in there, some food and kid's books is all."

"Better than nothing. Take the car back and tell Jacko we're coming in with the van" the leader instructed. "We'll do these two and then head back." He added. His lackeys laughed and the one from the van trotted off to a silver car at the far end of the street.

"So. Who the fuck are you?" the leader asked as the car headed off towards the opposite end of the village.

"Just passing through my friend. Nothing to concern yourself with" I said as I regained my breath and received a blow to the head from my captor.

"We aren't your fucking friends" he snarled into my ear.

"Ok. Sure." I said, head ringing.

"We were just looking for some food" Pat spoke quietly.

"So you were gonna steal our food?" asked the leader.

"We had no idea it was claimed I assure you. If we had then of course we would have left it alone." I told him raising my hands in what I hoped was a placating gesture.

"Well you did take it so now, we are going to have to punish you" said the leader, a grin stretched across his face. His lackey laughed along. I cocked my head to the side, I was sure I had just heard something beyond the laughter. Realisation dawned. I would need to stall a little.

"I don't suppose you are recruiting are you?" I asked the leader who just sneered.

"Why the fuck would we want you." His lackey laughed. "Tell you what though. Tell us where you have been staying and who else is with you and we might kill you quick."

"What makes you think we live anywhere other than the van?" I asked.

"You are too clean to be living in a van. You wouldn't need kid's books if you didn't have some people stashed somewhere" He said. Clever bastard.

I could hear a scrape on the path behind me. I concentrated on making myself as small as possible. "Well sorry to say boy, but we are not going to tell you anything" I said with a grin.

Leader's face flushed a deep red and he opened his mouth to speak just as the newly risen Mike fell on my captor from behind, his teeth sank deeply into the youths shoulder ripping through the material of his hoody.

Released from his hold I pushed myself to the side grabbing the baseball bat as it fell from the limp hands of the youth and flinging it towards the leader all in one smooth motion. The bat missed and banged against the side of the van as the gang leader ducked. The knife removed from his throat Pat leapt to his feet and began raining blows about the young leaders head and shoulders in a rage.

The screaming from my captor had been finally silenced. I darted in and grasped my hatchet from where it lay on the floor. "Thanks pal" I said to zombie Mike before burying the hatchet deep into his skull.

I pulled the blade free of Mike's skull and crossed to the leader who lay bleeding and battered on the floor. Pat sat beside him breathing heavily, the rage seemed to have left him.

"Kill him and let's go." I said to Pat who stared at me in shock.

"We can't kill him!"

"Why not? He was about to kill us." I replied.

Pat just sat and shook his head from side to side. "It wouldn't be right. He's alive. We can't kill someone who isn't a zombie."

"You might not be able to but I certainly can and will." I said, proving my point by chopping down with the hatchet against the young leader's neck. He made a few strange gurgling sounds and frothy blood spilled from his mouth as he died.

"What the hell!" Pat shouted.

"If we let him live he would come after us and the girls. Do you really want scum like this to get hold of Rachel or Ellie? What about Maggie?" I told him as I allowed a little anger to enter my voice.

Pat sat brow furrowed as he thought about what I had said. Finally he nodded slowly. "I thought you were taking care of Mike" he said as he climbed to his feet.

I shrugged. "Figured I had a little more time before he rose. Glad I was wrong." I said with a low laugh. "He saved our asses."

I picked up the bat and handed it to Pat before I retrieved the leader's knife. "Take the bat, you could use a weapon. We better get back to the others. You want to drive?" I asked.

We climbed into the van and I sat in the passenger seat perfectly content to let Pat do the driving so long as I could tell him where to drive. After a brief discussion we decided to leave the village after taking a look at the supermarket. We were in no state to raid it just yet but it would be useful to get a lay of the land first.

The drive was silent which suited me fine. Pat was lost in thought and concentrating on traversing the narrow streets. I was happily thinking about the people I had just killed. It was a different feeling when you hunted someone, trapped them and killed them at your leisure. I felt that could get used to this new type of pleasure I felt at killing in the open.

"Shit" said Pat as he brought the van to a stop. The street had been steadily rising as the village rose up against the side of a small hill. On the other side the road led down to the supermarket. From our vantage we could see the large brick single story building sat at the end of the road which led into a car park that stretched along the front of the store. On the western side of the building I could see the loading bays with a large security fence enclosing a small compound. A separate road led from the gates along the floor of the valley. The area before the supermarket was teeming with the undead.

"There. Look there." I said and pointed at the enclosed compound. The car we had seen driven away by the youth earlier was parked inside the fence. It seemed we had found the looters base. "Head back the way we came before they notice us." I instructed.

Pat rapidly got the van turned around and we sped through the village. We now knew why the village had so few zombies. The supermarket was lost to us and we wouldn't be able to get anything from it. We needed to rethink our plans.

It was getting late by the time we pulled up at the dirt track that lead to the farmhouse. With rain once again falling in a light drizzle that threatened to get worse, we decided to leave the supplies in the van. We picked out a couple of books to entertain Maggie and trudged on up to the house.

We were greeted enthusiastically by the five girls, all sat at the table in the kitchen. The joy quickly turned to tears for Rachel and Ellie as Pat informed them quietly that Mike had been killed. Rachel was in tears and being comforted by Claire and Ellie as Pat went to sit in the living room to dwell on things alone.

I handed the books to Maggie and was rewarded with a large smile. Lily moved around to stand beside me. "What happened out there?" she asked with a touch of suspicion.

Quietly I explained everything we had found at the petrol station and the shop before explaining that whilst Pat and I were in the mobile library Mike had been investigating the pub alone. I told her with all the sincerity that I could muster, that I had gone to find Mike and found him just as the zombies broke through the door. Pat had returned to the kitchen and confirmed what I had said.

Lily's gaze softened. Eager to move on I told her what had happened with the group of youths. She was understandably concerned by the implications. When Pat told her how I had killed the leader of the group I froze, my eyes locked to hers. All of a sudden my mouth was dry and my heart was beating faster.

Lily gave Pat a hug and then leaned in close to me. "It's ok. You were protecting all of us." She whispered as she put her arms around me and enfolded me in a hug. A wave of relief washed over me. She didn't consider her rules broken. I tentatively returned the hug before pulling back.

"We do have one rather large problem." I said to the group. I explained what we had seen at the supermarket, making sure that they all grasped the fact that there were likely more looters out there who weren't afraid of killing us for whatever we had.

As darkness fell beyond the farmhouse Rachel went to her bed to weep softly in privacy. Pat and Ellie sat together on the couch talking quietly and Claire was readying her daughter for bed. Maggie ran over and threw her arms around my neck and left a kiss on my cheek. "Thank you for the books" she said in her quiet voice.

Lily and Claire both laughed at the blush that filled my cheeks. It was not as unpleasant a feeling as I had previously imagined to actually be cared for. It was a strange feeling for me, but I actively wanted to protect these people. Lily handed me a cup of hot tea and we sat in companionable silence as the light faded and evening drew in. For a little while I was content and at peace sat quietly with a friend.

The quiet of the evening was broken by the sound of glass as it shattered and the screams of pain from Ellie in the living room. I jumped to my feet and dashed across the kitchen, Lily close behind. Ellie rolled on the floor of the living room wreathed in fire. Pat had a blanket in hand as he tried to cover her and douse the flames.

Beyond the smashed window four dark shadows stood in the night shrouded yard. One held another bottle in one hand and a lighter in another. He ran around the side of the house. More breaking glass and an explosion of light and heat from the kitchen as another flaming missile flew inside.

"Get upstairs quick!" I shouted as I ran to retrieve my hatchet from the kitchen. The table in the centre of the room was ablaze. Shadows danced across the walls and ceiling, the light from the fire removed any chance of seeing beyond the kitchen door. I edged carefully around the table and managed to grasp my weapon.

Pat was carrying Ellie's shrouded form up the stairs. Lily followed coughing from the smoke that was rapidly filling the room. I caught up with them at the top of the stairs. "Gather the others" I shouted to be heard above the panicked calls from the rest of my group. I pointed at a window at the end of the hall. "Get them to there. It opens above the stable."

"What about the bastards out there."

"I will deal with them, you get everyone to safety." I said, my voice was cold and firm. A darkness was spreading within me. These people were mine. This place was mine and someone had dared to attack it, the peace I had been feeling earlier fled before my cold rage. I turned to the window with a smile. I would meet them in the dark with a weapon in hand. I would be in my element.

The window opened outwards and looked out over the stables. I stepped onto the ledge and leaped down the four feet to the roof and then down to the muddy yard. I landed with a squelch of mud as a dark shape came around the corner.

When he saw me he raised a cricket bat and ran at me screaming. I jerked to the side as he swung the bat down and struck out with the hatchet. The back of his skull caved in with a satisfying crunch and he fell limply to the ground.

I picked up his bat and stalked to across the yard. I poked my head around the corner. The other three stood clustered together laughing. I counted weapons. A metal bar, a knife and one had managed to find a sword. It looked like a katana, likely some replica looted from some collector.

    A deep breath and then I stepped around the corner. The knife wielder saw me and called out to his companions as he loped towards me, metal bar wielder just behind. I flung the cricket bat low towards the knife wielder, it bounced off his shin and he fell to the mud with a curse.

    Metal bar wielder sprang over his friend and I advanced to meet him. He swung the metal bar towards my head. I ducked stepping beneath his swing and hacked his leg viciously. Blood flew from the wound and he screeched a high pitched wail. As he fell I slashed the hatchet blade across his throat.

    A chop to the side of the head took care of the knife wielder as he struggled to rise from the mud and I was left facing a young man holding a sword. Blood covered my hatchet and arm. I stood and felt it slowly run down across my fingers to drip against the floor. The sword man stared at me with wide eyes. I grinned and sprang forward.

    My foot slipped in the mud and I was suddenly falling backwards to land in the yard. The swordsman lifted the sword above his head in both hand ready to slash down. In desperation I threw the hatchet towards him. A sickening crunch was followed by a yelp of pain and spurt of blood as his nose broke. He staggered back one hand clutched to his face.

    I scuttled backwards to regain my feet before leaping once more at him. My arms encircled his waist and we fell together in a heap. The sword fell from his hand as he hit the ground. We rolled through the mud trading blows. Eventually I gained the upper hand as he slipped, feet scrabbling in the mud for purchase. I lay across his back and pushed his face down into the ground. I held him as he struggled to breath, pressing down with all my weight and strength. His struggles became more frantic before finally he was still.

Lily led the others around the building and stopped as they saw the carnage I had wrought. I looked up to see Pat cradling Ellie, still wrapped in a blanket. Claire holding tight to Maggie with her face pressed away from me. Rachel stood wide eyed staring about as Lily slowly approached me.

She crouched beside me and tentatively reached out a hand, slowly she placed it on my shoulder as if afraid I would bite. "Ryan." She said quietly, voice soft and calming. "Let go of him Ryan. It's ok."

I blinked, confused before I realised that I still had my arms locked around the man beneath me.

"It's ok. Come on, let go." Lily continued speaking softly as she took my arms, pulling gently.

I released my grip with a groan. Heedless of the mud and gore Lily embrace me gently. "Come on. We need to go." She whispered voice gentle and comforting to my ears.

Slowly I pushed myself to my feet and looked around. The farmhouse was burning, flames licked from the ground floor windows and a thick black smoke boiled into the sky.

"It's that guy from the village" Pat called across the yard. He pointed at the knife wielder with one foot. I nodded suddenly tired and not trusting myself to speak as the emotions surged within. I had killed them all, I wanted to leap and shout with exultation. I wanted to curl up into a ball and sleep away the bone weary ache I was left with as the adrenaline fled my body. I wanted to weep for reasons I could not hope to put into words.

Lily picked my hatchet up from the mud and passed it to me. "Let's go." She said taking my arm and leading the way across the yard and onto the muddy path. Our companions followed along, silent and tense. We reached the van which sat where we had left it. The silver car we had seen in the village earlier was parked behind it.

Lily climbed into the driver's seat, Claire sat beside her with Maggie cradled in her lap. Rachel helped Pat lift Ellie gently into the back and they sat together holding onto her as she whimpered in pain. I climbed into the back and closed the door behind me. I sat beside the back door as far from the others as possible.

I saw Maggie peering over her mother's shoulder at me, when she saw me looking back she quickly buried her head in Claire's shoulder scared. A little girl, all innocence and joy hid her face from me in fear. I slowly lowered my head into my arms and closed my eyes.

Printed in Great Britain
by Amazon.co.uk, Ltd.,
Marston Gate.